MW01614671

A Manx Daisy Chain
and other stories

Jane Davis

This work has been produced using a print-on-demand (POD) service. This means that the text or cover print quality may be variable. If you have received a copy of this book which is illegible or where the cover print is crooked or blurred, please contact the POD platform (e.g. Amazon) you purchased it from.

First Printing: 2022

ISBN 978-91-527-2764-5 (print version)

Contents

Foreword

The seed for this book came from an unusual advent calendar, consisting of a different sachet of tea for each of the first 24 days of December. Each sachet bore a brief description of the unnamed author's memories or experiences of Christmas. And for some reason I had the idea of a writing challenge based on these tea sachets.

The rules were simple. I had to write for at least 15 minutes. I could, and often did, write for longer, but I couldn't stop writing before those 15 minutes were up. And I had to take one or more of the words from the tea sachet as my starting point.

I've done this type of challenge before and it's amazing how inventive your brain can be under pressure. Give me a clear subject and a long deadline and I'll produce precisely nothing. Give me 15 minutes and a couple of words as a prompt and the words just flow and the stories leap and soar from one new world, one new character, to another. It's fascinating.

This time it was even more interesting because my very first story turned out to be set on the Isle of Man, where I was born and grew up. And several of the other stories followed from it. This book consists of that daisy chain of loosely interlinked stories, plus the tangled leaves and flowers of other Manx tales, and a few stories not set on the island.

In these pages, you'll encounter witches of many types, together with spaceships, mermaids, a robotic dinosaur and more than a few of the Isle of Man's own supernatural creatures, from bugganes to fairies – the Lil' People themselves.

The Isle of Man is a very special place; not quite British nor yet belonging to anyone else. It was Celtic, then Viking, then a mixture of the two, before becoming Scottish and then finally English. It has the oldest continuous parliament in the world and its own language, Manx, a Gaelic language that was considered to be dead when I was a child but is now very much alive. It has many myths and legends. And it has an incredibly beautiful and diverse landscape into which those myths and legends are indissociably woven like a single piece of tapestry. You can't have Peel Castle without the Moddhey Dhoo – the infamous and terrifying Black Dog – and you can't have the Moddhey Dhoo without Peel Castle.

If you've never visited the Isle of Man, you may find it hard to imagine how so much variation can be packed into such a small area (about 220 square miles, or 570 square kilometres). There's a spine of bare hills up the centre, and a large flat plain in the north – "down north," as my Granddad Corlett used to say – and a ring of wooded glens running down to the sea all around the fringe of the island. Sandy beaches on the northern coasts, pebbly ones down the east, tall cliffs near the southern tip. There's a castle made of limestone and one made of sandstone and plenty of slate cottages in between.

As a child, of course, I thought all of this was normal. It's only looking back that I realise how the Manx influences swirled around me like the currents of the sea. Growing up, I explored as much of the island as I could reach, on foot, by bicycle, by train and by tram, and later by car. My parents each in their own way imbued me with a love of the island's history and geography, and have each published books relating to the island. My paternal grandparents owned and rented houses in many different parts of the island, several of them at the same time! The cottage on Groudle Head was one, and the most isolated house on the island – up on the hills at the very top of the Druidale road – was another. The latter makes it into one of these stories.

I've lived away from the island for many years, and it's changed a lot since I left – rarely for the better. But I can trace my Manx ancestry on my mother's side back to at least the 15th century, and even though these days I'm a European first, Swedish second and British third (thank you, Brexit), it's still often the place I mean when I say 'home'.

So I'm very happy to bring you this collection of stories, and I hope some of them will find a place in your own mental landscape.

Jane Davis
July 2022

A Manx Daisy Chain

Explanatory note

Many of the Isle of Man's traditional folktales include the exploits of little old ladies that readers of Terry Pratchett would recognise immediately. A lot of them seem to be named Nancy.

A witch or wise woman would have been very important in a place like the fictional village of Lonaby, which was too small to have a doctor of any kind. Disputes would have to be settled, minor ailments remedied – both human and animal. And in every generation someone had to know how to do these things, just like the blacksmith passed his knowledge onto his sons. Even today, if you visit one of the smaller Manx villages, like Maughold or Ballakilpheric, you can imagine how isolated such a place would be when the only available transport was a horse and cart.

What may be a little less familiar to British readers is the character of Krampus, a goat-like figure said to visit children on the 5th of December, punishing those who have been naughty in the preceding year by beating them with birch rods. Meanwhile, St Nicholas is rewarding good children with gifts of nuts or oranges.

But no self-respecting witch would have any truck with that kind of nonsense going on in *her* village...

Old Nance and the Pie

Lonaby was a peaceful village. The cottages were always neat and tidy, with never a straw of the thatch out of place, the young men and women always had a cheerful word for any passer-by, and the children played their games of spinning tops and hopscotch without any of the squabbling you'd see in Douglas, or even in nearby Foxdale.

There were many explanations given for this calmness. It was said that the place had a favourable climate, and it was true that, nestled in a hollow on the flank of Slieau Whallian as it was, the village was sheltered both from the east wind and the soft rain that fell so plentifully on the rest of the island.

Some said there was a charm on the place, and indeed women would come and pray and weep and leave small gifts of flowers or a bit of cheese or a good herring at the foot of the old grey stone by the smithy, stroking its twined cross design like it was the head of the child they wanted or had lost.

And some said it came from the contented, gentle nature of the Lonaby folk themselves. Fine to look at, they were and strong, and bright eyed and open of face.

But Old Nance knew the truth of it, as she'd learned from Old Peggy before her, and as she'd teach to the one that would come after her.

In early December every year, she got the men to dig out a big fire pit near her cottage. And every year she had them lay in it a huge iron plate that took four strong men to lift it. And every year she got the women of the village to make a vat of pastry as big as a pig, and to prepare taters and carrots and onions. And once they'd done all that, and all that was needed was the meat, she'd send them away while she finished assembling the pie by herself.

There was always grumbling at the work, but it was always good natured, because Old Nance had delivered most of them as babies, and saved many a child from the flu or a broken leg, and she was always there if the cow fell ill or a girl was sick in the mornings and no husband at her. So they complained a little but they smiled as they did so, and asked her what would be in the pie this year. And every year, she'd say, "Well, you'll just have to wait and see, won't you?"

So every year on the sixth day of December, the whole of Lonaby came together at the end of the day, with bright torches burning, and laughter and singing of songs, and they'd sit at the tables in the village hall, all lit by candles and lanterns, and the priest would give a blessing.

The delicious smell that had been wafting through the village all day would get stronger and stronger as the men bore the huge iron plate, resting on beams of wood and still hot from the coals, into the hall from the cooking place. And then everyone would eat their fill of the pie.

And somehow, every year, nobody wondered how Old Nance – whose legs weren't what they used to be – had managed to get hold of so much goat for the filling of the pie.

Anna's Discovery

Anna Corlett was six years old when she learned that not everyone could make things sparkle.

An only child, and living in a remote farmhouse on the slopes of Beinn-y-Phott with just her mother and father for company, Anna didn't often get to meet other children. But lonely she wasn't, as she always stoutly told anyone who asked, for didn't she have the sheep her da raised, and the chickens her ma kept in the farmyard, and couldn't she talk to Jess the sheepdog whenever she wanted? Except when her father was out moving the sheep from one place to another, or bringing them in for shearing with Ned Cowell from over at Injebreck.

But when there were no sheep near and the chickens were all busy with their pecking and their worriting, Anna would skip down the path to the stream and sparkle things. She'd look at a twig, or a piece of sheep's wool caught on a fence post, and she'd do a kind of twist in her head. And in the next instant the twig would be up and marching around with a handful of its fellows, making a rigid little figure like the toy soldier she'd once seen in the window of a shop in Laxey, all fine and shining with a bright red uniform at him and boots as glossy as you could see your face in. Or the wool would be floating around over the short grass like a tiny cloud, with raindrops falling from its downy underside.

Anna was a truthful child, so when her mother Jinny asked Anna what games she'd been playing, she often said she'd been making things sparkle. But it wasn't until one wet Tuesday that her mother finally took notice of what she was doing. Anna often played outside in the rain, but this was a heavy drenching downpour and she couldn't go out in it no matter how many times she peeped out of the window and sighed. Eventually, she got so bored of watching her mother rolling pastry while the bread rose under a cloth by the fire that she sparkled the dough in the mixing bowl. Instantly, it leaped out onto the flagstone floor, in a series of little round squishy balls that tumbled over and around each other,

Catching the movement out of the corner of her eye, Jinny shrieked once, briefly, then to Anna's amazement waved her hand at the dough balls skipping flourily around on the hearthrug – and they all stopped. Just went from sparkled to still again, not gradually slowing down like they normally did when Anna told things to stop sparkling.

And then Anna's mother smiled at her and wiped her hands on her pinny and said, "Well, now, I'm thinking you and I need to have a little talk about this before your father comes home. And next week you and me will pay a visit to your Great Aunt Nancy in Lonaby. It's been a while and I'm thinking she'll want to see what a fine big girl you've grown into."

The Fairy Bakery

Down in the narrow back streets of Douglas, not far from the quayside and the Market Hall, you'll find a baker's shop. Or maybe it'll find you.

Because sometimes it's on the corner, where St Martin's Lane meets James Street. And sometimes it's right along near the Royal Hotel. And other times it creeps all the way down towards the railway station, so the passengers arriving from Peel or Ramsey or Port Erin have their nostrils full of the warm smells of fresh loaves and spices even before they've filled their eyes with the sights of the town.

But the scent is one thing, and it's a rare islander who gets to taste the bakery's wares more than once in a lifetime. Many's the man gone mad trying to find his way back to that door – green, it is, some say, while others swear upon all the Saints' names that it was blue or black or red.

If you've once tasted their goods, you never forget. But it's not that other bread or cakes taste worse for the comparison. Indeed, even the poorest of bonnags baked a week since still has something of the wondrous about it, if once you've tried the bonnag from the Fairy Bakery. For 'tis run by the lil' people right enough – or they have a hand in it somewhere, most folk agree, for all that the women behind the counter seem human enough.

And are, to hear them tell it, though they'll never speak of how they came to work in the bakery, or what kind of folk them that own it are. Nor even how they go about finding their way to work in the morning.

Breesha Kinrade worked there for many a year, with her sleeves always rolled up and broad forearms strong as a man's from kneading the dough. And young Jinny Moore, she with her hair as red as the autumn bracken, who would decorate the gingerbread figures fine as kings and queens, until she went off to be Jinny Corlett up at the farm on Beinn-y-Phott.

Fine steady women, all of them who work at the Fairy Bakery, and it's a lucky man who gets one of them to wife, for they bring good fortune with them as a dowry. And once a man's in right with Them Ones, he's set for life.

A Determined Woman

Breesha Kinrade was not a fortunate lass. A plain girl, she grew into a plain woman, and at the age of 18 she caught the attention of Juan Cregeen, a plain man with a passion for nothing but the fish he brought up from the depths of the sea. Out on the water on his boat, the Sea Queen, he was as happy a man as ever lived, but on land he was sullen and prone to fits of bad temper, particularly when there was a storm brewing and he couldn't get away from the shore.

Breesha bore with his surly ways and shouting as well as any woman could. And certainly he never raised a hand to her. But there was no love in their small house near the shore at Gansey, not between man and wife at least. He loved his boat, and she loved her baking.

For Breesha could make dough that you'd swear doubled in size the moment she left it to rise, and her bread was as light and fine as they'd eat in the dining room at Great Meadow, or even at the Governor's table. But she baked only for herself, for her ungrateful husband and for the folk around who were too old to knead their own dough. They'd bring her the flour and maybe a little something extra for her trouble and Breesha would make them a fine loaf or a bonnag all gleaming and golden, and everyone would be happy. Even Juan tolerated her baking, because doesn't even a fisherman need a full belly?

So Breesha was blessed with a talent but unhappy in her man and the poor cottage that was all they had to keep them warm at night.

And then one day on a trip to Douglas to visit her sister Ealish, who worked in a big draper's shop, Breesha found herself in a bakery that sold the most delicious biscuits she'd ever tasted. Aye, you know the one: the Fairy Bakery. Because that place chooses them that will eat its wares. But it also chooses them that will serve behind the counter.

Well, the long and short of it was that Breesha soon found herself working there, and it was a terrible long way from Gansey to Douglas, even with the train from Port St Mary. But Breesha was happy. She loved serving the customers – a strange, bewildered lot most of them were at finding themselves in the Fairy Bakery, but always so grateful to taste the delicacies she suggested might suit them or theirs. A fine pork pie with glistening jelly might mend a broken heart, while a twist of pastry light as air would do as much for an ailing child as any tincture the apothecary could concoct.

And what was even stranger was that Juan didn't seem to begrudge her the time spent away from their own hearth. True, she was bringing in wages, and that helped make their mean cottage a little more welcoming, for they could afford coal from time to time to supplement the peat for the fire, and real wax candles too. But he seemed to be more cheerful even than these little additions could warrant, and Breesha was puzzled as to the explanation.

Until one day the Douglas train broke down just outside Colby, and seeing that there was no help for it that day she turned around and walked home. She didn't mind the walk at all, for it was a fine bright autumn day. And when she thought of it, she wasn't at all surprised to find her husband sitting on the bench outside their cottage, laughing and singing as only a man deeply in love can do, while a mermaid sat on a nearby rock, combing her long dark tresses and smiling sweetly at him.

Juan jumped up guiltily at the sight of his wife, but the mermaid simply paused for a moment in her brushing and looked boldly at Breesha, then carried on admiring herself in the looking glass.

Breesha folded her arms and glared at the pair of them, but before she could utter a word Juan spoke with fierce determination. "I'm going to the sea," he said. "I'm going to live beneath the waves with Mona here and never come back on land as long as I live."

"Indeed, and I'll not be giving him up," said the mermaid swiftly. "For it's plain to see you don't want him, leaving his house all cold and dark all day and no one to pour the tea or keep the fire burning." Breesha wondered exactly how the mermaid was going to pour Juan's tea or stoke the fire under the water, but she'd learned at her mother's knee that there was no arguing with a Ben Varrey. And, she realised, she felt no inclination to do so.

Instead, she went silently into the little cottage and gathered together her few bits of things – her mother's Bible, and the little wooden cat she'd won at the Tynwald Fair as a child, and the smart hat Ealish had given her last Christmas, and made a bundle of them and her scant other clothes. She would come back with Simon the carter for her dresser and her fine china another day. Just now she felt nothing but relief at being freed from her marriage. For a husband lost to the Ben Varrey is as good as dead, and no blame at all on the wife who can't stop him from leaving.

She took one more look around the inside of the cottage, then went out and gazed steadily at the mermaid, still smoothing her shining black locks, while Juan looked on nervously. And before she walked away to her new life she said, "I wish you well of my husband, for he's been precious little comfort to me. I hope he'll be more use to yourself."

The Sweetness of the Land

Once upon a time there was a little mermaid called Cara, and she lived with her mammy and her daddy and her sister Mona in the clear Manx waters off the shore at Port St Mary. Well-named was Cara, for the word means someone who loves to sing, and from the moment she was born Cara was always humming one tune or another.

As she grew older, her happy songs of the sea spray and the beautiful pebbles on the seabed changed to wistful airs of love, for Cara was mightily taken with Patrick, a merman who lived amongst the rocks down below Bradda Head. But Patrick was a handsome young chap with flashing dark eyes and gleaming dark hair, and he had many mermaid admirers leaving him pretty seashells and longing glances wherever he swam.

So Cara would sit on her favourite rock, off the shore at Gansey, and sigh and sing and sing and sigh, and all the while she would think of Patrick. Or envy the luck of her sister Mona, who'd been so fortunate as to find a human man to love and who loved her back. Often such matches failed, because the ways of them beneath the sea were strange to humans, and the ways of humans very stiff and unfriendly to them beneath the sea. But it warmed the heart to see Juan and Mona together in their cosy little undersea grotto, his tender glances and her making his tea over the fire that burned so brightly with mermagic. Cara often wondered if she wouldn't do better to find a human man herself. But the heart can't be driven with reins and whip, as me old granny used to say, and she'd begun to think she'd never find a way to capture Patrick's affections when one day she *did* meet a human man.

For the little cottage near the sea that had once belonged to Juan and his human wife was empty no longer. A man had come to live there – a solitary man, with no wife at him, and his back quite bent with age, but he seemed no less happy for that. Indeed, he sang almost as much as Cara, but always bright and happy tunes, as he toiled at a row of boxes set amongst the potato patch.

His voice was so fine, and his joy so evident, that eventually it roused the sad young mermaid from her sorrows and she joined her voice to his in harmony. The man looked around, startled, for a moment before his eyes alighted on Cara and he returned her smile even as he kept singing.

When they reached the end of the song, he walked carefully to the edge of his garden where it became more water than land, and bowed politely.

"A fine morning to you, Mistress," he said, "and made even finer by the pleasure of hearing you sing. My name is Eamon. And your voice is as sweet as the honey my bees produce, though I'm sure many have told you this before."

Cara smiled, then sighed. "Thank you, sir," she replied, bowing in turn as much as her seated position allowed. "Cara is my name. Though I know not what honey might be, and the one I wish to admire my voice the most seems unmoved by it. But it gave me pleasure to sing with yourself too."

"Is there no honey beneath the sea, then, Cara?" Eamon asked. And when she agreed there was not, he bustled off to his little cottage, which had a fresh coat of limewash and was as spick and span as any home could be, with the bees all buzzing peaceably around the gorse flowers.

Eamon returned with a large jar, and removing the lid he dipped a small spoon inside, bringing out a golden substance that was not quite liquid like water nor yet solid like stone. He stepped cautiously on each of the large boulders that led to Cara's rock on the edge of the deeper water, and passed her the spoon, twisting it deftly so the honey would not fall onto her iridescent, scaled tail.

Even before she brought it to her lips, the scent of the gorse blossom surrounded her and she smiled in delight. And then the taste! For wondrous though it is to be able to live at the bottom of the sea, there's no sweetness there as we have in our apples and blackberries...or our honey.

Cara was charmed by the flavour, and that night when she returned home she could speak of nothing else to her parents. She visited Eamon several times in the next few weeks, and each time they sang while she sat on her rock and he worked on his hives or tended the potatoes. And Eamon said the bees were producing even more and even finer honey than they normally did, and that it was all due to Cara's sweet voice.

When she next saw Mona, she told her all about her new friend and his beehives and the wonderful stuff they produced. And Juan overheard and looked melancholy for once as he never usually did. "Oh, honey," he sighed mournfully. "Indeed an' I do miss honey."

And Cara was very fond of her brother-in-law and wanted him to be happy, so the very next day she swam back to the rock near Eamon's garden and waited for him there, singing a song that was a little more cheerful than was her wont.

At last he came around the curve of the track, carrying a chair roped on his back, and looking a little warm, but when he saw Cara waiting for him, he smiled broadly and strode towards her as if unbothered by his burden.

"A fine day to you, Mistress Cara," he said. "I've brought meself a new chair, but 'tis an outdoor chair so we can sing together, if that would be pleasing to you. For I'm not as young as I once was." And he proceeded to untie the chair from his back and place it down near the water's edge.

"Oh, how lovely!" exclaimed Cara, clapping her hands together as she admired the fine sturdy woodwork. "An' I'm wondering if you could give me a little honey to take home to mammy and daddy and to Juan and Mona, for they've heard tell of it and they're awful keen to try it themselves."

"Indeed and I can," said Eamon, "I thought of exactly that meself while I was at the market today fetching me chair, and I got a little pot with a lid on it that I'm thinking won't let the honey out under the sea."

So Cara swam back that night with some golden honey in the little pot, and Juan's face was a wonder to behold. And Mona found it just as good, and even better the next day when Cara made honey cakes using a kind of flour cunningly ground from sea anemones.

Cara shared the cakes with her parents and all her friends, and instead of her having to swim after Patrick, he was now often to be found near to where she was, so pleasing did he find the sweet flavour.

But as to whether he learned to appreciate Cara's sweet voice and temperament as much as Eamon did – well, that's a story for another day.

To Charm a Witch

There's some who say you've never lived until you've witnessed a Manx wedding, from the blowing of the cow's horn outside the bride's home the evening before, to the procession to the church, and the feasting and drinking that follows the service.

Imagine, then, how much grander a spectacle it is when the wedding takes place beneath the sea! Aye, for the finery of the guests and the wedded couple is wondrous to see, and the procession escorted by seals and fishes of all kinds, and the horn is a twisted thing from a gigantic sea monster, with the booming it makes fit to wake Manannan himself if he's not sleeping sound.

And there's the rub. Stormy weather when a lass from Sulby weds is bad enough. But when the bride is a mermaid and she's wedding a lad with a tail as fine as her own...then the sea must needs be flat calm if the garlands aren't to be washed clear to Ireland.

And so it came about that Patrick the merman from under Bradda Head had a keen desire for fine weather one day in June, and according to the custom of his folk he decided there was nothing for it but to visit Kirree the witch at Castletown.

Now Castletown has a fine harbour, and it was no problem for Patrick to swim in past the castle and into the shallow water beyond, but after that he had to strip off his scales, as all merfolk can when they wish. He climbed onto the land and tucked the tail part neatly behind a creel, dressing himself in an old fishing net, which mermagic transformed into a fine suit of clothes. Then he walked briskly on his own two feet, first into the town where he made some purchases, for there's so much treasure lost at the bottom of the sea that a merman is never short of a little gold. And then he carried on until he reached the windmill where Kirree lived, in a cottage kept tidy by the folk all about, who were greatly afeared of her magical powers and even more so of her short temper.

He found Kirree at home, and no more in charity with the world than usual, sitting on the bench outside her cottage and squinting at the mill sails spinning around and around, and smoking her pipe.

"Good day, mistress," he said, all fine and handsome as only them from under the sea can be.

"Tis nothing of the sort," she retorted, knocking her pipe out on the bench. "'Tis a nasty chill sort of day that will only bring rain and winds to follow it." For Kirree was a clever woman as well as a witch, and she could see as soon as looking at Patrick the kind of man he was, and what his errand must be.

Patrick was downcast, for if the weather wasn't fine he wouldn't be able to marry Cara, and he did so want her for his own bride and no more waiting to be done. Then he remembered the gift he'd brought, and he smiled at the witch and said, "But it could be a fine sweet bright day today, mistress, no matter the sky."

The witch frowned at him but she hadn't lived near on three hundred years by interrupting people carrying small packages wrapped in brown paper and tied up with string. Not least because a witch is always curious, and often hungry, but also because it was market day in Castletown, which meant fresh white bread, if not cake too.

So she bade him continue, and with the air of a conjurer – for all merfolk are apt to be showy in their ways, so handsome are they – he pulled from one package a fine purple shawl of softest lambswool and with all lacy edging around it, and spread it out on the bench beside the witch. Then, one by one, he placed the other parcels down.

"Ye can open them ones too," said Kirree, "and mind you don't crumple the paper." For brown paper is very useful to a witch, for poultices and such. Or even for writing charms on, I've heard.

So Patrick set to opening the gifts he'd brought.

One was indeed edible – a handful of vanilla biscuits, all sweet scented and crumbly with sugar, and Kirree was of a mind to grant the merman's wish straight away, for those were her favourite. But she could tell from his air that there were greater things to come, so she held her tongue, which is a fine skill in anyone and even more rare in a witch.

Next, there was a little bunch of woodruff and ferns, fetched from the woods around Silverdale and as fresh and green-scented as a spring morning. And then there was a fine old book with maps of all the countries in the world, with scenes from each land on the pages between, for Patrick knew that witches are great travellers, even the ones that never leave their homes.

And then there were just two gifts left: a tiny parcel of seaweed tied off with a bit of twine, and a fine large white envelope.

Kirree's finger hovered over the envelope, but she read in the droop of his shoulders that she was to keep that one to last, so she pointed to the smaller present.

And Patrick placed it on her palm and pulled away the twine. Inside it was a piece of sea glass all worn smooth by the waves and never a hand to shape it, not since it had been part of a bottle many years since. Blue, it was, and you'd have sworn it was made as a likeness of Kirree's own blue cat, just now sunning himself on the garden wall and waiting until such time as fish or milk might be forthcoming.

"Now them's mighty fine gifts already," said Kirree a little suspiciously. "So what is it you're wanting from me that there's another one?"

"Your...your pardon, mistress," stammered Patrick nervously, his assurance deserting him at last. "I'm not for flattering you without reason. Them's all gifts right enough, and this last one is something of a gift, and something of a blessing, I'm hoping."

And seeing that the witch was becoming impatient, he hurried on. "I'm to be wed next Saturday, and I've heard you can make it so the weather is fine for my bride. For she means as much to me as all the treasure in the sea."

Kirree grunted and sat back on the bench, working the knots out of her back.

"Aye, that I can, if I'm so inclined. And you've done enough thinking and talking before coming here to ask me, what with me favourite colour and them pretty flowers and me favourite biscuit and a little cat like my own fella there. So you go inside and put the kettle on and we'll have a nice cup of nettle tea – for its wondrous good for the blood – and maybe a vanilla biscuit. And we'll talk about your wedding."

And three days later, Patrick and Cara were wed under the sea, and the water was calm and smooth as a mirror, and it's said you could hear the singing and music clear up to Peel.

Oh, but you want to know about Patrick's last gift to Kirree? Well, when he opened the envelope, it contained an invitation to the wedding. A human bridegroom would never think of bidding a witch, nor writing her name, but them under the sea have different ways. So although she'd been to many a wedding before, this was the first one Kirree the witch had ever been invited to. And go she did, wearing her purple shawl, and she danced that long and that hard that even the porpoises were tired trying to keep up with her.

A Touch of Spice

Now the reader who's been keeping up with my little tales will be thinking there's no bad ones and never a cross word spoken on the Isle of Man, and that all it takes to turn a man from surly to cheerful is the right woman. And there's some truth in that right enough. But the island is a place like any other, with joy and sorrow and some that'll never be happy no matter where they are in life.

And one such was William Jowett, and it wasn't just that he was an Englishman in Mann that made him cross – though there's enough about the place that makes them brought up to different ways gnash their teeth and tear their hair.

No, this Jowett was as mean-spirited and miserable a one as ever lived, and he'd have the coat off a starving man's back sooner than give him a little longer to pay what he owed. For Jowett was a moneylender – that's to say he worked for the Bank in Castletown, and he made it his business to know everyone else's business and find ways to charge them for it.

Well-known in the town he was but not well-liked, for all that he had a fine big house out by

Derbyhaven, and a whey-faced wife, and two boys at King William's College, and plenty of servants to make life easier for him.

And so one day Kirree the witch, fed up of hearing the townsfolk carrying on something awful about this Jowett, decided to do something about him and his penny-pinching ways. She went to the Bank, all neat and tidy dressed as she could, leaving her blue cat and her tall hat and even her witches' broom at home, so them in the Bank didn't know but that she was just an ordinary old woman.

"Come to pay me respects to Mr Jowett," she said to the clerk on the desk, "and brought him some of my own home-made gingerbread, the good it is that even a fine gentleman like Mr Jowett has never tasted its equal."

The clerk wore a very white shirt with a very stiffly starched collar under his jacket, and this was apt to making him cross and unhelpful to all those who asked for his aid – and isn't that always the way with the sad folk doomed to dirty their hands with the business of the Bank? But the smell of warm ginger coming from Kirree's basket was so tempting that he thought he'd better tell Mr Jowett in case he heard tell – as he surely would – of this wonderful gingerbread and how it had been refused entry to his office.

So the clerk went and told Mr Jowett and in the shake of a duck's tail, Kirree found herself in the finest room she'd ever seen.

"Sure and you've an office finer than the Governor himself," she exclaimed, turning around and around to admire it, while the scent of the gingerbread wafted out to fill up even the far high corners of the room.

And Mr Jowett, seated behind his enormous mahogany desk, couldn't but feel hungry, even though he just eaten the four courses that was all he allowed himself in the way of lunch.

Presently, Kirree stopped her examination of the room and sat on the mean, narrow chair meant for visitors, placing her basket on the desk and beginning to rummage in its depths.

"Here we are now," she said, removing the biggest, boldest and above all tastiest-looking gingerbread man Mr Jowett had seen in his life. "This is a gift from me to you," she said, "to show you my admiration for all you do for all of us poor ordinary folk here in Castletown and all around."

Mr Jowett smiled his thin smile and nodded his peevish head and he may have even uttered a word or two. But in the next instant he was clutching that gingerbread man in his hands and biting and chewing and swallowing and biting and chewing and swallowing as if he hadn't eaten for weeks.

Kirree looked on with a smile as he ate, and soon it was all done and Mr Jowett was using a finger to chase the last of the crumbs around on his shiny black trousers.

"V-very good," he finally managed to squeak, as the warmth of the ginger spread throughout his body. And not just through his body either, for it seemed as if the warmth of the spices had made their way into his head too, and everything seemed just a little brighter and more pleasant than it had a moment before.

"Well I'll be leaving you now," said Kirree briskly, standing up and gathering her basket.

"Oh but must you rush off so soon after giving me this delicious gift? Surely you'd like some tea, or coffee perhaps? We keep some for our very best clients, you know, and you are definitely that, dear lady. Or perhaps I can lend you some money?" He leaned confidentially over the desk and whispered, "We have such a lot of it here, you see, and I often think it must be a lonely and boring life for all the notes and coins stuck down there in the vault all the time with never a glimpse of daylight or the chance to change hands."

Kirree thought it was just possible she'd overdone the special spices, but it was too late now and anyway he'd been asking for it, so she declined politely and went on her way. And from that day on, William Jowett was the most jovial and charming of men to everyone he met. He lent money to all those who asked for it, and he might have got in trouble with the Bank's owners excepting that Kirree had a stern word with the townsfolk. "I've sorted the bank man for ye," she told them. "But you'd best not be taking advantage of him, for if ye do they'll be sending another one – and worse – from Douglas to replace him."

So Mr Jowett's loans were always repaid on time and his head office was happy with him, and so was his wife, seeing him so much more generous and ready to please than before. His servants, too, his horse and his cat and his dog all thought him greatly improved. Only his sons, come back from school for the holidays, thought him altered for the worse, for they were already well on the way to becoming bankers themselves.

The Widow Mylchreest's Garden

Now it so happened that in those days there was a buggane living on top of South Barrule. And this buggane wasn't a bad feller, for all his size and his huge teeth like gravestones and his eyes as big as the roundabout at Tynwald Fair and spinning twice as fast. He kept to himself, by and large, and only took the odd sheep when he was really hungry, which wasn't often, for he was getting on in years as even bugganes do in the end.

But he had a terrible thirst at him for the drink, and he was no more careful than you'd expect once he'd drunk a barrel or two of whisky.

And this mightily displeased his nearest neighbour, an old widow woman who lived in the hollow there just where the Ronague Road runs over the Round Table and across down to Dalby. Widow Mylchreest she was called – for though she must have had another name once she'd long since forgot it. She'd been married to Ned Mylchreest who for many years was a fisherman out of Port Erin. But when the sea took him one stormy January night, she vowed she'd never live within hearing of the water again, and so she moved herself and all her possessions right up there on the hills where the only things she could see, she'd say to anyone who'd listen, were "the sheep, the hills and the Lord himself."

But for all that she was a praying woman she tolerated the old buggane most of the time. Two old folks together, they were, and many's the time you'd pass before her front gate and see the pair of them sat up against the wall of her cottage, sunning themselves or having a chat or enjoying a good thick slab of bonnag with white Manx butter on it.

As well as her baking, the Widow Mylchreest devoted her time to her little garden. All hedged about with neat stone walls, it was, and as full of flowers and pleasant smelling herbs as any apothecary could wish.

So you can imagine her dismay when one night there was a terrible crashing and shrieking all around the house, and how, when she emerged from under the bed where she'd taken refuge in fright, she found her little garden all smashed up and with giant footprints everywhere.

It was pretty clear what had happened. Two days before there'd been a wedding down under the sea off Bradda, and the music and singing had carried on all the while since. The Buggane must have been invited – or at least invited himself, for there's not many brave enough to tell a buggane that he may not do something. And on his way back he'd got himself all tangled up with her garden wall and thrashed about until he'd found his way out again.

"Indeed and me garden'll never be the same again," she said sadly, beginning to clear up the wreckage and see which of the plants could be saved and which there was no hope for.

She wasn't angry, for she knew that anger at what you can't help just eats away at you from the inside like a worm in an apple. But she did regret not picking her raspberries the day before when she could have enjoyed them instead of them being squashed flat by the buggane's huge hairy feet.

While she was working, she heard a familiar thumping noise coming down the hill behind, and soon the Buggane himself was looking over the garden wall with a very woebegone expression.

"Did...did I do all that?" he asked hesitantly, and his whirling saucer eyes span even faster than normal in his shame.

"Aye, me dear, you did, and I'm thinking it must have been a grand party for you to have been in such a state."

"I'm terribly sorry Mistress Mylchreest, indeed I am. And your poor flowers trampled and everything." And he looked as if he was about to weep.

"Nothing that won't grow again," she said briskly, even though many of her plants had taken a long time to raise.

"I'll put it to rights," said the Buggane. "You see if I don't."

"I'm sure you will," said the Widow Mylchreest, though she didn't really believe it, for a buggane's hands are not made for repairing a flower garden, any more than they are for knitting a shawl.

But the old woman had forgotten how a buggane lives a good long time and makes many acquaintances – both friends and enemies – during those long years. And this buggane had been an amiable sort, by and large, and had a good many favours owed.

Sure enough, the Buggane let it be known that he needed a hand – or rather many small hands. And the next day when the Widow Mylchreest got up and opened her curtains, she saw such a scurrying and rushing and a flurriting that she had to rub her eyes to make sure she hadn't imagined it.

There were new plants everywhere, fine flowering beauties and the biggest vegetables with the glossiest leaves you ever did see, and herbs of all types too and even a rosebush of the special type called 'Governor's Lady', which she knew for a fact only grew in the Bishop's garden.

And all about them were crowds of lil' people, pushing and pulling and digging and directing with such boundless energy that it made her feel tired just to watch it.

So she closed the curtains again and sat by the fire quietly singing sea shanties to herself until the rustling and bustling outside had stopped. She'd rather have sung psalms, but Them Ones tend not to be too keen on those, and she did want her garden back.

Finally, there was a big sigh, then a ripple of fairy applause, and then a rushing noise as of hundreds of tiny feet skipping away, and then silence.

And then the sound of the Buggane's heavy tread and his careful knock on the door.

"'Tis all done, Mistress Mylchrees'," he said, when she opened the door. And indeed it was, as pretty as a picture with hollyhocks and peonies and delphiniums and all the things you'd want in a cottage garden, and even some you'd never think of on the Isle of Man, like a young palm tree and a walnut and a fig, looking all the more exotic for being surrounded by the bleak moorland.

"Well *they'll* never take," she said with her hands on her hips. "And if they do I'll be long gone before they fruit. And what's this?" And she pointed to a candle standing in a little lantern, fixed atop the wall. As she turned she could see there were more of the candles, all around her garden wall.

"They're to light me way," said the Buggane proudly. "When I'm off out I'll light them for ye, and then I shan't be crashing through your garden again."

"Hmm," said the Widow Mylchreest, though secretly she thought it a good idea, and like to make her garden an even prettier place after dark.

And indeed it was – and not just after dark, either, for those three trees all grew tall and bore fruit the very next year. And the Widow Mylchreest's coconut, fig and walnut loaf was eaten and talked of in those parts for many a year to come.

The Miller and the Mill-Hand

Did you ever see Tommy Corlea, him they always called 'Little'? No? Well he wasn't one of the lil' people, for all that he was short of stature. No, Tommy was just a very short man, half the size of his brothers and not even up to the shoulder of his shortest sister. But he was brave as a lion, was Tommy, and nobody ever got the better of him.

Well, maybe the once, aye, that's true enough. For Tommy was a mighty close man in some ways. He'd give you his own dinner if you let on that you was hungry, but if he thought you were trying to cheat him or take advantage he could be tough as nails. And that made him a hard employer to please.

And so it came about that Tommy was looking for an assistant to help out at the mill he ran down there near Ronague. For he was selling a great deal of flour in them days, especially to the Widow Mylchreest, for she was doing a powerful lot of baking.

But he couldn't get anyone he liked the look of, for they was all too skinny or too fat or too old or something. And all the fellas who'd been mill hands before had gone off to work in the mines at Foxdale, or to Laxey to work in the big new mill there, or even in the mines there under Ruari Moore, so he couldn't get anyone with experience, and the ones he tried without it was worse than useless.

And Tommy was close to giving up and thinking of selling the mill when one day this fella came up to him as he was walking home, and he said, "Tommy Corlea, I'll be your mill-hand and the best one you've ever had, and I won't take any wages for a whole month, nor will I."

"Work for a month with no wages?" said Tommy. "You must be mad. Or a fool."

"No, I'm not mad and I'm no fool," said the stranger. "All I'll take at the end of that month is the flour I can grind for you in an hour."

At this, Tommy looked hard at the man, suspecting a trick. But the stranger had an honest, open face for all that he was black haired and blue eyed and a bit too handsome for Tommy's liking.

"One hour's worth of flour for a whole month's worth of work?" he said.

"Aye," said the other.

Tommy turned the proposition over and over in his mind, but he had little choice for he needed a mill-hand something terrible and he'd already tried all the likely candidates nearby – aye, and many of the unlikely ones too. So he agreed and they shook hands on it.

The stranger's name was Adam, and he certainly was a good worker. No sooner did he set foot in the mill than the sacks of flour were fairly flying out, and finely ground it was, so fine that you could make a loaf of it that would almost float out of the oven it was so light.

Early every morning, Adam arrived at first light and set to work, and every evening as the sun was setting he'd tidy everything away, bid Tommy goodnight and stride off into the darkness.

It got so that Tommy was buying in grain from the north of the island to keep up with Adam's toiling. But he could sell this fine quality flour for a ha'penny more per pound, so he was well pleased overall.

Soon enough the end of the month came around and Adam came to Tommy and said, "'Tis time for my wages, and then I'll be on my way for I'm of no mind to stop at one job the rest of my time."

Tommy was very surprised at this and tried to get Adam to stay by offering him a proper wage, and even to put him up in his own house, but Adam wouldn't change his mind – and just as well, too.

For when he began to run the mill for his own wages, Tommy realised the stranger had only been working at a fraction of the speed he was able. He shovelled the grain and flour like a madman, filling up hoppers and sacks in the blink of an eye. And the mill stream seem to pick up on this urgency, rushing down through its channel at ten times the rate it normally would until Tommy was fearing it would carry the big mill wheel away with it. Aye, and it was a close run thing –the mill gearing was near enough to setting alight, it was spinning around that quickly, and the bitter smell of charring wood came pouring out from the machinery as fast as the flour.

Tommy could only wring his cap between his hands and watch the mill heaving and groaning and wheezing like an overworked horse. For it was obvious enough that Adam was no ordinary man, and watching the speed he was working at Tommy began to suspect he might even be dealing with Old Nick himself.

Then suddenly it was all done, the hour was up and the old mill stood there, steaming faintly in the sunshine and all creaking and clanking as it slowed down and stopped.

And the one who had said his name was Adam winked at Tommy Corlea and picked up all the many, many sacks of flour he'd ground, all at once somehow, and tossed them up onto his back and said, "Thanks to ye, Tommy Corlea," and walked out of the door of the mill. But when Tommy bethought himself to run after him, there was no one there in the mill yard at all but the cat, slinking along with his fur and ears all flat.

Well, from that day on Tommy Corlea was a much more suspicious man, but a much fairer employer and he never had any problem getting a mill-hand again.

And what would the Devil do with all that fine white flour? Well, nobody knows for certain, but it's true that the lights were often seen on the fairy mound at Ballagilbert that year, and always accompanied by a delicious smell of baking bread.

How Laxey Got Its Wheel

You'll have heard of the bugganes I'm sure – them fellas that stamp around the island, roaring and making a fuss when they don't get their own way. Aye, they're a terrible noisy lot, and if you live near one it's as well to become accustomed to the row and stay on his good side, or he might take it into his head to have the whole roof off your house, like that one did with St Trinian's Church.

But not all bugganes are male – well, if you think about it, they couldn't very well be, could they? For all they're not human folk, still they come from somewhere and aren't just hewn from the rock in the quarry there at the Dhoon.

Now the female bugganes are rare and shy creatures, on the whole, for all that they're just as huge as their menfolk. But there was one such – Ysbal was her name – who made so much of a racket that the whole town of Laxey was struggling to get a night's sleep.

She arrived in late summer, and all through the autumn she'd sit up the valley there, just above the town, spinning away on her wheel that was tall as two men, making gigantic balls of yarn from straw or reeds and sometimes even whole hazel trees. All the while she hummed a little song that was loud enough to make the plates on the dressers shake as far as the Snaefell Mine, up under the foot of the mountain. And always at night, for bugganes are nocturnal creatures and not fond of being out in the daylight.

And Ruari Moore, the Captain of the Mine, was unhappy, for his miners were all sluggish and half awake all day on their shifts down in the ground. Now, a sleepy miner isn't a safe miner, and 'twas a miracle there wasn't a serious accident while Ysbal was spinning away at the autumn's harvest. And, as the women of Laxey said, what would happen when she finished her spinning and took to knitting, with the clattering of needles bigger than tree trunks?

One night, lying there wide awake in his bed for the third night running, Ruari decided that something had to be done. Being a wise man, he knew the best way to deal with a buggane – any buggane, but particularly a female one – was to call upon an even wiser woman. And so the very next day, without even waiting for his breakfast, he was off on his horse to Lonaby near Foxdale, to see Old Nance.

Now, if you've the island's geography clear in your head, you'll know that Lonaby's a powerful way from Laxey, and you'll perhaps be wondering why Ruari didn't ride to Ramsey to talk to Lilee the witch instead.

But here's the thing. Ruari was from the Moore family there at Greeba, and they've always had strong women in that line. His sister Jinny had something of the power about her too, but Jinny had chosen to be married and have a daughter rather than follow the witches' path. For 'tis not an easy one at all.

Whatever the way of it, when Ruari arrived in Lonaby after a long ride, you can imagine his disappointment when he found Old Nance away. Only his young niece Anna was there, 20 years old and apprenticed to Nance the last three years, for magic will be where magic will be.

"I'm sorry Uncle Ruari," said Anna, on hearing of his problem. "She was fetched this morning by the Governor's man to help with something. Very pressed to be away, he was, and very tight-lipped, and the long and the short of it is that Aunt Nancy's away to Douglas and only me here. But I'm near to finished with my 'prenticeship, she says, and maybe I can help you?"

"Well, I don't know about that, Anna. A buggane's a powerful thing, and I wouldn't want to make her angry and have her rampaging about the town and destroying the houses. And what if she damaged the mine workings?"

"Indeed, Uncle Ruari, and I'm no longer a child," said Anna indignantly, with her hands on her hips and her eyes flashing so that Ruari could quite easily picture her in 30 or 40 years as Old Nan, ruling a village with a will of iron. "Bugganes and phynodderees and all them craythurs are all a one. They need to be taught their place, that's all."

She began bustling around the small cottage, collecting a bottle of this and a pouch of that, a rod of hazel and a handful of sheep's wool, and several things Ruari couldn't put names to at all. Again he suggested it would be better if they waited until Nancy was back from the Governor's business, but Anna said that could take days – or longer – and he did want to see the back of the buggane before she drove the whole town to drinking.

In five minutes Anna was ready, with her sturdiest boots and cloak on, and carrying a little sack with all the tools of her trade. So Ruari pulled her up behind him on his horse, and they began the ride back to Laxey.

It was coming onto evening when they arrived, and Ysbal was spinning away on her wheel, and humming fit to burst. Bugganes may have many fine qualities, but the ability to hold a tune isn't one of them. So what had been merely unpleasant when they rounded the last corner on the coast road became more and more discordant the closer they rode, until eventually as they reached Ham and Egg Terrace they had to dismount from Ruari's fretting horse and leave it tied to a post. The instant their feet touched the ground, they could feel the thump-thump-thump of the spinning wheel turning, with Ysbal's enormous foot on the pedal.

"Well uncle," said Anna, raising her voice to be heard over the racket, "I can see why it is that you want her gone. For 'tis a terrible noise. And it can't be doing the town any good at all, not the people, not the chickens nor the dogs and cats, not the cream in the pot." She rummaged in her sack and produced a couple of scraps of cloth which she tore up. And they set off to walk the last few hundred yards with bits of cloth stuffed in their ears to stop the hullaballoo from shaking their brains to jelly.

As they went, Anna bent and scooped up a couple of handfuls of mine tailings, all sharp little bits of rock left behind from when the metal had been extracted. She stuffed them in her pockets and they carried on the last few hundred yards to where Ysbal was sat with her spinning wheel as tall as two men, a-humming and a-thumping fit to burst.

But bugganes do have some manners in them, especially the females, and she stopped when she saw the two of them approach, and rose and made a clumsy curtsey.

"Good evening to you, ma'am," said Ruari, doffing his hat, for he was a polite man, even as Anna made a hmphing noise beside him.

"And to you sir and lady. 'Tis a fine evening for spinning," boomed Ysbal cheerfully in reply, picking up a sapling from the heap beside her and making as if to carry on with her work.

"I was wondering," said Ruari, a little emboldened at this exchange of courtesies, "whether you might perhaps do me the favour of taking your spinning wheel a little further away from the town? Only your terr...your wonderful voice is keeping people awake."

Anna shifted impatiently beside him, keen to show her prowess in the banishing of Them Ones. And she didn't have long to wait.

"Awake?" howled Ysbal, much offended. "Awake, aye, and they should be awake, all sleeping all the night and doing their work in the day! 'Tis a terrible lazy way to be going on, I'm thinking. And I'll not be moving anywhere! Indeed, I'd been thinking of asking a few of me friends from down Jurby way, and having a bit of a natter and a sing-song. That'll learn yous people to be lounging in your beds all night." And muttering, she busied herself with tidying up the vast skeins of yarn she'd spun from the bits of branch and reed and tree lying in the heaps around her.

Now Anna stepped forward, and said, "If you please, Mistress Ysbal, I've heard that the folk at Garwick are even lazier than here, and they certainly need to be woken from their slumbers."

As you might expect, this wasn't true, for there was nobody in residence at Garwick at all in them days, but Anna knew she should give the buggane one more chance to leave with dignity. Old Nance had taught her well that it was always best to find a peaceful solution if possible, rather than immediately resorting to witchcraft.

But sadly Ysbal was a stubborn one, and she was having none of it.

"Indeed and I shan't be moving," she roared. "I have me things here and I'm stayin'."

At this, Anna stamped her foot and shook out her wrists. "Indeed and you are not stayin', for there's none of your things here." And with that, she chanted something Ruari couldn't catch, and flung out the scraps of tailings from her pockets – aye, and a few other things she'd put in her hands too, I'm thinking – and suddenly there was a creaking and a rustling from all around them, and the heaps of vegetation that Ysbal had set aside for spinning began moving of their own accord, with the poor withered roots seeking out the soil, and shrivelled leaves unfurling and becoming green and glossy again. The ferns sprang up in thick clumps around the base of the spinning wheel, the saplings formed a living fence all around it, and the creeping plants began to grow in and around the spokes of the wheel, preventing it from turning.

And Ysbal the buggane was first struck speechless and unable to move, and then as the iron in the mine tailings began to have its effect she gave such a howl that the glass in all the houses in the town cracked in its frames. And she gathered up her skeins of yarn in a huge basket and thundered away up the valley. And that was the last that was known of her, although for many years afterwards folk from Jurby often heard strange thumpings and howlings in the night. So perhaps she'd gone to meet her friends there.

In any case, Ruari was relieved to see her go. He turned to his niece to congratulate her, but her expression was not a happy one. And looking at the buggane's spinning wheel, he could see why. Anna's spell had stopped it spinning, right enough, and it was now overgrown with vines and creepers and trees. But it was also twice as big as it had been before, and still growing, with the vegetation creaking and snapping and writhing to keep up.

"What is it that's happening?" he said.

Anna looked astonished. "Indeed I don't know, Uncle Ruari," she said. "I've done that spell a hundred times before, and it's always behaved itself."

The wheel was now six times the height of a man, and the top of it was towering over the greenery surrounding it.

Ruari looked frantically about them, as if somehow the bare hillside would provide an answer. But Anna was calm. For witches are problem solvers at heart, and it wasn't the first time she'd made a problem worse before it got better. As the wheel grew still more, and Ruari began to worry that it would squash the whole town before long, and the mines underneath too, Anna stood there counting things off on her fingers.

The noise of the wheel expanding was immense, but he could still catch the odd word. "Fennel, yes, and...valerian... fingers...and...TAILINGS!" she shouted. "It must be! Too much iron! Uncle Ruari, is there much iron in the tailings here?"

"Well...yes," he shouted, trying to pull her away from the foot of the wheel. "Zinc, we mine zinc, but there's iron in the tailings of course, I have an assay in the..."

"No time!" she shrieked, and turning to the encroaching bulk of the wheel, which was now 12 times the height of a man and looming over them, she shouted something and made a gesture in the air.

And suddenly, the tremendous noise of the growing wheel was gone. All they could hear was the creaking of stressed vegetation, the crunch of settling earth and the chatter of worried voices from all around the town.

"Well," said Anna, stepping back and taking a deep breath. "Now I know why Aunt Nancy tells me I must pay more heed to the soil and not just the things growing in it."

And indeed, she was a wiser witch after that night – aye, and one with a much keener interest in geology, too.

Now I'm sure you've already guessed what happened to the wheel. It stood there for a while, all overgrown with plants and trees. And then one day one of the mine engineers had the idea of using it to draw up the water from in the mine so they could dig even deeper.

And even now, the Laxey Wheel is the biggest working water wheel in the whole wide world. It has another name too, for it's also called the Lady

Isabella. There's them as'll tell you it was named after the Governor's wife. But now you know the truth – that it was named for its previous owner, Ysbal the buggane.

A Shape in the Mist

If you've ever visited the fortune teller at Tynwald Fair, you'll know how it goes. You pay your money and the fortune teller brings out a green glass fishing float and tells you you'll meet a tall dark stranger – or maybe a short fair one – and before you know it you're back out on the grass in the bright sunshine quick as if Them Ones had magicked you there.

Well, when Molly Joughin went to the fair with her Maddrell cousins from Greeba it was no different. Her and Tom Maddrell saw the fortune teller one after another, and they both had the same fortune – they were each going to meet a stranger very soon. Only when Molly was leaving the tent, the fortune teller took hold of her wrist and hissed, "Listen! You must listen!" But when Molly asked what she must listen to, no answer did she receive. The cousins could make neither head nor tail of this, but there were so many wonderful things to see at the fair that it was soon forgotten.

They were sat on the grass, taking turns at drinking lemonade from a bottle with a marble in the neck, when Molly saw her friend Aalish in the crowd. Childhood friends, they'd been, but Aalish's parents had moved to Peel and they'd not seen each other for a year or more. The two girls were very happy to be reunited, and Tom was even happier to meet the newcomer for the first time. Aalish was a pretty girl with red hair and blue eyes and fine white teeth, and Molly soon realised that Tom was talking only to Aalish, and she to him in turn.

And some time later, when Molly set off to leave the fair with the rest of her cousins, Tom was nowhere to be found. "Gone to walk some pretty maid home to Peel," said his mother indulgently. For Tom was her favourite. He was back home late that evening, blushing and smiling and keen only to discover from Molly all that she knew of Aalish. She shared her knowledge willingly, for Aalish was an amiable girl and just the type to make a good wife for Tom.

In the morning Molly set off for her own home, ignoring the road and heading off up over the hill, past the mill and up onto the moors. For 'twas only a couple of mile to her own home on the banks of the Colden stream. Born and raised on them hills, Molly was, and she'd been running wild up there from the moment she could walk. But on the Isle of Man the weather is apt to play tricks on you in the blink of an eye, and she soon found herself in a thick mist, barely able to see two paces ahead of herself.

She'd known where she was when the mist came down, but if you've ever been in that kind of weather yourself you'll know well how every step can take you off your line, and how before long you can no longer say if you're going uphill or down.

And so it came about that Molly was soon as lost as she'd ever been in all her 19 years. She wasn't afraid, for she knew it would lift before many hours had passed. But she still had her best boots on, and could no longer see well enough to stick to the dry areas. For it can be boggy and damp up on the hills even in summer. So she took her boots off and knotted the laces and strung them around her neck, and tucked her skirts up into her waistband to keep them out of the mud, and then she stood and thought for a minute.

If she could find a slope, one way or the other, she'd soon know where she was, as she'd just have to keep going downhill a way until she recognised some wall or fence. But there seemed to be only flat ground with bilberry bushes and scratchy heather, and between them muddy puddles.

In the end she set off towards a patch of the mist that was maybe a bit lighter than the rest. And she'd not gone far when she saw a dark figure some way ahead of her. She was that pleased to see someone she almost called out, but as she drew breath to do so she suddenly remembered the fortune teller's words. It was a tall dark stranger, right enough. But now she could see that the head appearing through the mist was that of a horse. She knew all the wild ponies on these hills and this beast was far too big to be one of them. But perhaps she could ask the rider which way she was headed.

Only...there was no rider, nor even a back for a rider to sit astride. And when she listened, as the fortune teller had told her to, she realised she could hear only one set of feet splashing across the boggy ground.

Her blood ran cold, and for a moment she thought she'd drop in a dead faint, but then she turned and ran. Just ran away. Away from the glashtyn – the half-horse, half-man creature she'd heard of since she was a little girl but never thought to meet.

She didn't stop, she didn't look back, and she managed somehow not to fall over in her flight. And soon enough she recognised a wall and then a tree and then another and before long she was in her mother's kitchen, telling the story between great heaving breaths.

Now, later that day the mist cleared, and Molly and her father went back up on the hills to see what they could see. Plenty of footprints there were, of both man and horse – and possibly of glashtyn too. For who knows what Molly saw? There are certainly many more things up there in them hills than you might think, sitting in your nice warm home in the town.

The Three Sisters

There are many trees on the Isle of Man, and as many stories associated with them. But the one most Manx people know is no kind of plant at all – 'tis a number. For in the language they speak on the island, the number three is spelled "tree."

'Tis said to come from the Vikings who once lived here, and who brought their language with them when they decided to settle and stay here all year round rather than just raiding the place in the summer. But whatever the reason, it's a fine number, and not just because of the famous three legs of Mann either. For it wasn't so long ago that the best known three wasn't the symbol at all, but the Three Sisters of Injebreck.

Nowadays Injebreck is a bit of a bleak place, away up there in the hills and either drizzling and damp or blinding sun or howling wind. And in truth when the Three Sisters lived there it wasn't much better. But they liked their own company, and they loved the hills and the big skies above them, and the sweet mountain air with just the sound of the sheep and the skylarks for neighbours.

They had a neat white cottage in a hollow about where the plantation is now, and a vegetable garden that they grew in the old way with long rows of raised soil, and bladderwrack added to the one fallow bed every three years.

But they didn't just live on the produce of their own little bit of garden, for the Sisters had come from a good family in the south of the island once, before they made their home at Injebreck, and they still had a bit of money at them for all they'd set their faces against their kin. Some said it was because they'd been found husbands they didn't love. Others said they just didn't want to live a life of duty and manners, for such was the lot of a genteel lady in those days.

Whatever it was, here they were, renting a cottage from James Corlett, one he'd been sure he'd never find a tenant for. And a repairing lease too, so when they took possession the place was not much better than a ruin, but in just a few weeks it had a new coat of limewash and a fine new stove inside on new laid flagstones and the chimney all repaired and cleaned, and the thatch as neat as a corn dolly. And then came the removals carts – for they had a fair few belongings too, and ye'd have thought they'd never fit all of it in the house, but 'twas all judged to a nicety and in it all went. Vases for flowers and dainty little tables and curtains of sprigged muslin and even a piano – only a small one, to be sure, but all the same, 'twas magical to be walking on the Beinn-y-Phott road over to Ballaugh or Kirk Michael and to hear Miss Alice tinkling away on it.

For all three of the Sisters had their own talents. Miss Alice was the musical one, who could lay her hand to any instrument and had a voice that could charm the birds from the trees. And she was greatly in demand for weddings and the like down in the lowlands.

Miss Moira was the artist, often to be seen sitting amongst the heather and stone walls of the high hills with her easel weighted down with a stone and her hat tied on against the wind with a bit of old string.

And Miss Eleanor could have been a pastry chef to the King of England himself, if only she'd have agreed to come down from Injebreck and compete with the other bakers in the kingdom, for there wasn't a one who could make lighter puff pastry nor do a more beautiful bit of icing.

They had suitors, over the years, for even up there in the hills there are others around, and word of their beauty wasn't long in spreading from the artisans who repaired their cottage. Many's the man who'd call with a posy, all dressed up in his Sunday best no matter the day. And some of them were received kindly, and treated to Miss Eleanor's delicious biscuits and kind enquiries as to his family. But just as often the would-be suitor would have his hand raised to knock on the door only to see the three of them flee in different directions from the back of the house, their long wild hair that never saw a comb floating behind them like banners, and their queer white dresses and overjackets they always wore concealing their forms like Mannanan's Cloak does the island against invading foes.

It could never be said whether they had something against a given suitor or whether he'd just come at a wrong time, for there was many a good man never got closer to the sisters than hearing their laughter as they slammed the garden gate and ran out onto the moors. And there was certainly no catching them once they'd decided they were away.

Some say the Three Sisters were witches, but I'm thinking they were just happier in their own company than pandering to a husband – and there's nothing wrong with that.

Fairy Footsteps

There was once a man called Ewan Kerruish, and he lived up near the top of the Sulby Valley, not far from where the Tholt-y-Will is now, if you know the place.

Ewan wasn't old, nor yet was he in the first flush of youth, but he was still as strong and agile as he'd ever been. He'd had a wife, but she'd died some years before, and he didn't much miss her for she'd a tongue at her as sharp as the thorns of a sloe. Now if he ever felt like hearing a woman's voice, he had but to climb the hill up to the house of the Three Sisters, there above up at Injebreck, where he always got a kind welcome and a bit of music into the bargain. But for all that, he was happiest in his own company.

So Ewan lived very peacefully there in the shelter of the valley with his goats and his spuds and his apple trees. But one summer he found he'd got visitors, and not the welcome kind either.

No, he was being favoured by the lil' people, and a particularly playful bunch too, for it seemed like every time he turned his back while the butter dish was out on the table, when he looked again there were tiny footprints all along the length of the butter.

Ewan was a tidy man and this vexed him sorely. So he got in the habit of putting the lid back on the butter dish the instant he'd taken some on his knife. And for a few days that put a stop to the footprints, but then one day he came in from milking the goat to find the lid of the butter dish smashed on the flagstones and that many footprints in the butter it looked like someone had been having a ceilidh.

So he thought for a bit, as he scraped off the top of the butter and fed it to the dog, and then he spread what was left on the good fresh bread he'd made that morning, and ate it, still thinking. And then he put on his cap and his best coat and called the dog and took his stick and set off down the valley to Quayle's Store.

Once there, he bought himself some more butter – which surprised Mrs Quayle greatly, as she'd sold him a whole new pat only the day previous – and a fine new butter dish with a pattern of primroses on, for he'd always liked their cheerful faces. He also purchased another item, all wrapped in a damp cloth to keep it moist.

And after smoking a pipe and exchanging a bit of skeet with them as was sat on the bench outside the shop, he set off back up the valley.

Back at his cottage, he laid out the butter dish and placed the new butter carefully in it. Then he unwrapped the big damp lump of clay he'd carried back from Quayle's and broke a bit off, kneading it between his hands until it was soft and smooth. And he laid it out in the old butter dish, for all the world like a grey slab of butter next to the white one.

Then he cleared his throat and said, "Indeed, yer welcome to skip about on this bit of clay, for it mus' feel good on yer feet, but I'd rather you didn't step in me butter any more, thank you kindly." And then he bowed, as if he was before the Bishop himself. And just in case this wasn't enough, he added, "And there'll be a dish of bread and goat's milk on the step every evening for ye to sup on."

He listened for a reply but heard nothing, not even a whisper.

But from that day to this Ewan Kerruish has had no more problems with his butter, and every week he takes the trampled bits of clay down the valley to Quayle's Store, and they're taken to Douglas on a cart and fired in an oven and painted bright colours and sold to the tourists as authentic souvenirs of the Manx fairy folk.

A Dancer's Escape

In the town of Ramsey, up there on the flat northern plain of the island, there are all kinds of shops. And at one time one of them was an antique shop. As you'd expect, it was full of quaint, interesting things. Cuckoo clocks and jewellery, dim dark paintings where you could hardly make out the subject, old walking sticks with carved heads, jugs and vases of all types – and all objects with a story to tell if only you had the ears to hear them.

Unfortunately, in those days the shop was run by one Mr Crellin, and although he liked to see old curios, he preferred to keep them on the shelves of his shop rather than sell them. He wasn't so hard up that he needed the money, and he owned the whole building and lived in rooms over the shop, so he had no rent to pay.

That meant he was very reluctant to sell any of the things in his shop, no matter how much money the prospective buyer offered him. The prices marked for each object were already extortionate, but if ever a customer agreed to pay such an enormous amount he'd look at the vase or necklace or painting or whatever it was and shake his head regretfully and say, "Now that it comes to it, I'm afraid I simply cannot part with it. No, it's much too dear to me to let it go."

As you might expect, many people were very cross about this because they thought he was just trying to get them to pay even more. But some believed him and offered him a still greater sum, if it was an object they particularly admired. Always in vain. Mr Crellin thought it was a very poor month if he sold a single item, and on the day our story begins he hadn't sold anything at all for a whole year! Every day he opened the shop, and every day, all day, he sat there behind his desk, admiring the beautiful objects around him, and every day he turned away all the customers who came in. This made him very happy, but it didn't stop him accepting more stock for the shop – no, indeed it didn't. Sometimes it was difficult to find space for it all, but Mr Crellin had come to be skilled at stacking it all up and squeezing in an object of just the right shape for a particular gap, just as if he was building a drystone wall.

Well, now, just like a wall, which shifts over time and finally gives way, it so happened that one night there was a bit of a collapse, and a few small things slid from the top of one pile and down onto the floor – or what passed for it, because it was several layers deep in Persian rugs, which didn't add to the stability of the furniture. Fortunately the rugs also prevented breakages, but a musical box that had been in the shop for at least 10 years and probably a lot longer landed on its side with its lid open, playing a plaintive tune.

The tune wound down after a couple of minutes, after which there was a brief burst of high pitched oaths from the box, and then a small figure climbed out of it and stood on the rug, stretching her back to get the knots out.

"Well," she squeaked, looked around at her surroundings. "I'm glad to be out of there and no mistake." This was, of course, the clockwork dancer from inside the musical box. She'd been shaken loose in the fall, but seemed to be none the worse for her ordeal.

Slender she was, blonde haired and blue eyed and with a long green dress the colour of the spring grass, with a golden tiara and a pair of white dancing slippers on her tiny feet.

Yet she stamped around on the Persian carpet as though she was a soldier on parade. An angry soldier. For she was most unhappy at having been kept imprisoned in the box for so long.

Because Fenella – a good Manx name given her many years before by a good Manx lass – loved to dance. She loved to see people smile as she twirled around in her box to the beautiful music. She loved to make people happy. What she didn't love was spending year upon year folded double in the darkness of her box, with only dust filtering in and never a mote of light nor a note of a tune.

She quickly scanned the antiques around her and, seeing a lighter patch that she correctly surmised was the front window, hitched up her gossamer skirts and started the long trek to the front of the shop – and freedom.

It wasn't at all a straightforward path, for she had to squeeze between table legs and clamber over pieces of broken stoves and door stops and old table legs, but eventually she found herself standing in the small clear patch by the door. It towered over her, and at first she wondered if she'd need to find another way out, but then she felt a draught and realised there was a letterbox cut in the door. It was quite low down, but even so she needed to jump up to reach the bottom edge of it. She dragged herself up into the thickness of the door, then pushed and shoved at the piece of wood covering it on the outside until the hinge finally swung out, and the letterbox spat her out onto the pavement.

It was still very early in the morning, and there was nobody around, so she wasn't worried about being seen by humans, but she could see a cat further down the street, stalking along and sniffing at everything. Now when she'd still been dancing in her musical box for the little girl who named her, Fenella had quickly learned how much cats love movement, and she had no great desire to meet another one. So she waited until the cat had disappeared into a shop doorway and, gathering her silky green skirt, ran as fast as she could across the street and into the alleyway opposite.

For as well as having a great appreciation for music, Fenella had a keen sense of smell. And the scent of fresh dough rising and ovens warming was very clear. She scurried along the alleyway, watchful for other cats – or even rats! – and careful of where she put her feet. And soon she came to another doorway, this one open, and wafting out a wonderful warm smell of bread.

She slipped inside the bakery quiet as thistledown, but there were two men talking and they wouldn't have heard her had she made ten times the noise.

"Aye, it's going to be a fine day, I'm thinking," said one.

"I'll be glad of it, for 'tis a mighty long way up to Injebreck, and a miserable trip if it's raining," said the other.

"And what do them ones want now that you're having to go all the way up there again?"

"Oh, they took a fancy to a dresser when they were here for the festival, and so I'm off up the mountain with that for them."

"A dresser, is it? Well it's a wonderful long way to go in a cart just for a few women to show off their fine china. I'd rather stay here in the warm and carry on kneading my dough," said the baker.

"Aye, but it's worth the trip to maybe get to hear Miss Alice singing," replied the cart driver.

"So I've heard. You'll take a few rolls with you for the ladies? Miss Eleanor was mighty complimentary about them, and her with a touch for the baking that would make you weep."

"Aye, I'll do that."

At the mention of singing, Fenella had stopped wondering how she could climb up onto the counter and try some of the wonderful smelling bread, and started wondering how she could climb up onto the cart and go with the driver to his destination instead.

She peered back out of the doorway. Sure enough, there was a horse and cart a little way along the alley. She slowly started edging back towards the door. Meanwhile, the baker went to a tray of rolls and popped a few of them in a brown paper bag, handing them to the carter, and saying, "Would you drop that sack of yesterday's bread off with the Joughins up at Claghbane on your way? They're raising pigs for

Christmas, and pigs are mighty fond of stale bread soaked in water with a bit of milk in."

"And a bit of pork for you in the bargain too, I'm thinking?"

"Aye, right enough!" As the two men laughed heartily, Fenella skipped back through the doorway and over to the cart. It seemed very high above her, but fortunately there was a bit of rope trailing down from the back of it, and it was easy to pull herself up and onto the flat wooden boards at the back.

There was a tarpaulin stretched over something – the dresser, Fenella assumed, so she found a way underneath it, and tucked herself up in its folds.

Soon the cart was on its way. It was a long journey, and a slow one, and not very comfortable either, for all that the road over the mountain was a new one. For cart travel is a jolting, unpleasant type of motion. But the day was fair, and after a little while of drowsing half awake, Fenella emerged from beneath the tarpaulin and sat on the boards, watching a huge wide world appear behind them as they climbed ever higher.

There was Ramsey near at hand, and the silver-blue of the river, and the curve of the coast, and green fields and small villages, and then in the distance a white church, and further beyond that even the land came to a stop and there was only sea and blue sky, with not a cloud in it. And after being imprisoned in a tiny box for many years, it was almost too big for Fenella to take in. But only almost. For she was a brave one, that little dancer.

"I'll never go back to that box," she said fiercely to herself, as the sweet-smelling mountain breeze ruffled her golden hair. "Never. Not if I can help it."

Soon enough, the cart turned off the mountain road, with Snaefell behind them, its top gleaming in the sunshine. And not long after that, Fenella heard the faint tinkling of a piano, drifting across the moorland grass and heather. It was playing a waltz, and Fenella couldn't resist the rhythm. On the back of that rumbling cart, all but losing her footing with every jolt, she twirled and swayed.

She was so caught up in the music that she didn't notice when the cart stopped, nor when the door of the cottage opened, nor when two female voices met up with the male one of the driver. Because the waltz continued, and so did Fenella's little feet, skipping from one side of the cart to the other, her green dress swirling around her.

She did finally notice, however, when the voices stilled as the people all caught sight of her dancing. Her steps faltered, and she didn't know what to expect. But manners took over, and she swept a graceful curtsey, holding her skirt to one side as she'd seen her former mistress being taught.

"Good morning to you," she said politely. And she was very surprised when the two ladies, both dressed in curious white outfits, both curtseyed back to her.

"A very good morning to you," replied the taller of the two. "My name is Eleanor, and this is Moira."

"How beautifully you dance!" cried the other woman. "I should very much like to paint you. I'll just go and fetch my pencils..." And with a flurry of skirts she disappeared back into the house.

Meanwhile, the cart driver was scratching his head and looking puzzled.

"I don't know where you come from, young miss, but I hope you haven't done any damage to that dresser."

"Indeed I haven't!" declared Fenella, stamping her foot. "I've not been near the silly thing, I just took a ride on the cart. And now," she said with a dignity more suited to someone of much greater stature, "I should like to get down, please."

Eleanor and the cart driver both looked about them as if searching for some appropriate conveyance, but just then another woman, also dressed in a flowing white dress and white jacket, appeared rather breathlessly at the back of the cart.

"Hello!" she said. "I'm Alice. I hear you're a very good dancer. Would you like to come inside? Perhaps you could dance on the piano while I play?"

And that was how Fenella the music box dancer came to join the household of the Three Sisters, right up there on the top of the hills.

She danced while Miss Alice practiced. She danced as Miss Moira drew her. And she danced as Miss Eleanor made delicious cakes and tarts, often decorated with the figure of a small dancer in icing or pastry.

And sure enough, she never again had to go back to her box.

The Fairy Market

You'll have been at the market in Douglas, I'm thinking, the herring and the cockles and all them spuds and cabbages. Aye, and cloth of all types and boots and pots and pans and all the china you could ever need. And the Fair at Tynwald too – there's not many on the island haven't been there and eaten toffee apples and drunk lemonade and listened to the speeches. And there's the markets in the other towns too, and sometimes the villages.

But I'd bet my best Sunday hat that you've never been to the fairy market – no nor even heard of it, I warrant. Unless you're one of the lil' people yourself, in which case begging your pardon, this is a tale for humans and no disrespect meant.

No, the fairy market isn't meant for men and women, but only for Them Ones and all the other magical folk of the island. For indeed, if you're a buggane and you're after ointment to keep your teeth all shiny, or a phynodderee in need of a comb, where can you find them? If you're a fairy wanting a new dress, where do you get the best fabric? You can hardly be strolling into Looneys in Ramsey and asking them behind the counter to help you pick it out now, can you?

So the fairy market's for other folk to sell to other folk. It's held in the big field at the foot of Cronk Sumark four times a year, at the solstices, and a great event it is each time. There's chestnuts and apples roasted in the autumn and flaming torches lighting the market field in the winter, all fresh flowers in garlands in the spring and delicious rhubarb and gooseberry fizz in the summer. And music and laughter and a great deal of talking, for Them Ones are a solitary lot as a whole and they don't get to chat with their neighbours like us humans. Indeed, for a buggane up there on the hilltop or a glashtyn down in the riverside reeds, 'tis an awful lonely life.

And at the market they can buy whatever they want – wonderful things such as you could never imagine, come from the fairy realms and the workshops of magicians and the cauldrons of witches. Cloaks of invisibility, love potions, magic swords and seven-league boots aren't even the half of it.

But as a mortal, you'll never see the market, nor hear it, not even if you pass right by on the road under the hill there. For we aren't all the same and we don't all have the same talents in life – and if we did it would be a mighty dull world, I'm thinking.

Old Things

There was once a lad called Aidan and he lived at Maughold with his grandmother Margid, for his parents had both died when he was a little boy.

Now Aidan had a good bit of learning at him, for he'd been to school until he was nearly 14 and his granny thought he should be off to Douglas to work in a big shop or an office or something clean where he wouldn't be out in the cold and rain all the time, but he was having none of it.

"Me da was a fisherman, and his da before him, and 'tis a good job for a man so that's what I've a mind to do," he said, standing there before the fire for all the world as though he was indeed a grown man and not still a scrawny boy.

Margid was afraid for him, going out there on the big wide sea, for she was a sensible woman and knew well that a thing's not to be conquered just for the wanting of it. But he was a stubborn lad, and so that first day she watched him off in the small boat he'd had from his father, and said nothing against it.

And indeed, the lad took to the sea as though born to it – for hadn't he been? He had a rare talent for finding the best fish, and soon enough he was bringing in enough for them to sell to the best fishmongers in Ramsey and to make a nice bit to put by. Or that's what Margid wanted to do, but Aidan insisted that she spend some of the money on doing the house out nice as she'd often spoken of while he was growing up.

"Indeed Granny," he said, "when I came to live with you I recall you'd paint me pictures with your words of what the house would be like when we'd made our fortune – all flowers in vases and a pianer and all them things you used to have when you was a girl."

And it was true that Margid had married beneath her when she'd wed Cormac the fisherman, her that was a Miss Cannell from one of the big houses up Bowring Road in Ramsey. She'd had to give up a lot when she moved to the little thatched cottage near the shore in Maughold, and she still thought fondly of those fine things.

So she let him buy her new linen for their home, and a smart new tin to keep their stock of tea in, instead of a rough crock pot. And bright new plates to stand on the dresser in place of the old cracked ones. But when he took down the little box she'd decorated so long ago with pokerwork, and looked with distaste at the fragments of knotted rope, ragged lace, worn wood and sea-smoothed glass inside, she spoke up.

"I shall keep that," she said in her careful way. "I think I may have a use for it yet."

"What use could anyone have for a bit of old rubbish like this?" asked Aidan scornfully. But when he saw she was serious he replaced it back on the shelf as careful as if it was the Crown Jewels, for Aidan was that fond of his old granny.

Well, it came about that he learned the use of that old rubbish soon enough, for a few days later he was out at sea when a storm came up out of nowhere – a witch-called storm, sure as anything – a storm fit to topple chimneys and rip the thatch right off your house if it wasn't tied down right. And Aidan trying to get into the beach with his catch but pushed back and towards the rocks every time.

After another fruitless attempt, he looked back at the beach in desperation and saw his grandmother standing there, arms crossed. He shouted to her – he didn't know what – but Margid just impassively watched him struggling then turned her back and went indoors. And, sure his time had come, he wished he'd done as she suggested and taken a nice easy job in Ramsey or Douglas instead of fighting the sea.

But Margid hadn't abandoned him – of course she hadn't. She'd merely gone inside to get her little box. She opened the lid and took the chain of old twine and bits of wood and glass in her hands, and then she stood there on the beach with the sea spray swirling all around her, and she spoke a few words... And suddenly, just there in that bay, in front of the shingle beach, it was if it was a different day. The storm was still all around, and the sky black as night out to sea and all the way up to North Barrule, but right in front of Margid and right out to where Aidan was in his boat there was a bright light like the sunniest of summer days, and the water was flat calm. Well, Aidan didn't need telling what he must do. He dug in his oars and rowed as quick as quick into shore and had the boat up on the beach before you could blink.

And then he gave his granny a big hug and they had two good big herring each for their dinner, and plenty of strong tea. And all the time, Aidan vowed over and over how he'd never again suggest they get rid of Margid's old things.

A Witch's Favour

If you've a few years behind you, you'll remember the old butcher's shops around the island. In Douglas, I recall one in Strand Street and one on the Terrace and one down in the row of shops near the cooling tower at Pulrose. They all smelled the same – of meat and the sawdust sprinkled on the floor. They all seemed to be run by large, cheerful red-faced men. And as well as sausages and chops they all sold things like brawn and chitterlings. And sometimes they'd sell potted meat. A prosaic name for a delicacy – at least to a child's palate – and made even more special by coming in a little white pot all of its own. And one of those butchers – and I'll not tell you his real name, for I promised I'd never say – had the recipe from a witch, and that's why it tasted so good.

How it came about was like this. At that time, the great grandfather of that butcher was himself a butcher's assistant, with no prospect of ever being anything more. And he was walking through a field out Lezayre way one day with his gun, for he'd been after rabbits. He'd been lucky, and he was carrying three fine fat conies over his shoulder as he strode towards home. And as he came up to the foot of the church, where in them days there was a little well to capture the fresh water from the spring, who did he see sitting there on the big stone by the well but Lilee the witch.

For in them days everyone knew who was a witch and who wasn't. Not like these days when anyone with a bit of book learning can call herself a witch even if she knows nothing about healing or the weather or the ways of animals.

"Well now Jem," said she as soon as he came within earshot. "I've been delayed caring for Peter Killey's cows all day and I won't get to the market before closing time. If you give me one of them fine rabbits for me tea, I'll make you a rich man."

Now, Jem had nothing against being a rich man, and he had no need of three rabbits, for two was more than plenty for him and his parents to sup on. And it never hurts to be in with a witch. So without further ado he unslung the fattest of those bunnies and presented it to Lilee with a small bow, as if he was giving the Governor's wife a posy.

And the witch laughed, and said, "You're a well-mannered lad and you'll go far by your own efforts, but come and see me in the morning and I'll give you something to help you along your way."

Well, Jem could hardly sleep all that night for thinking about what the witch might give him. Surely it would be gold or silver? For everyone knew witches could find buried treasure just by sniffing it out.

So you can imagine his disappointment the next day when all he got for his trouble was a recipe for potted meat, written up on an old scrap of brown paper. But you can't complain about a witch's behaviour – at least not to her face – so he took himself home and gave the recipe to his mother, saying nothing about where it had come from.

And when his mother made the potted meat, it was the tastiest thing any of them had ever eaten. So tasty that they ate the whole lot straight from the pan and she had to make some more to put into the store cupboard. And this time the smell of the cooking brought the neighbours around, and they swore it was the most wonderful good thing they'd ever eaten too.

Soon word spread and people were queueing all down the road for a sample of this marvellous stuff, and paying whatever Jem asked to get a bit spread on a scrap of bread. And so it wasn't long before Jem had the money to go to Ramsey and buy the old shop that used to be Mr Crellin's antiques, and have it all fitted out to make a butcher's shop all of his own – where he could carry on making and selling the witch's potted meat to all the folk of the north of the island – aye, and some from the south too!

Other Stories

The first of these stories is also set on the Isle of Man, taking a more contemporary look at witchcraft in the 21st century.

The other pieces vary in length from a Drabble (exactly 100 words), through flash fiction to several thousand words, and from romance to SF. They were primarily written in response to prompts from writing workshops or specific markets. Some are fragments, rather than complete stories.

A Rite of Passage

The handle of the broomstick plunged half a metre into the sticky mixture of water, mud and reeds, nearly taking Kerry with it. Again.

Already covered in mud, and more than slightly redolent of semi-rotted vegetation, Kerry swore. That made almost half an hour in the labyrinthine wetlands of the Curraghs, and still no sign of the blasted water hemlock.

Maybe coming in from the east would have been easier? But no, there definitely been a good big patch of the stuff in this part of the Curraghs only two weeks earlier when they'd done the field trip out here. Or at least there'd been plenty *somewhere* here. One umbellifer growing in a soggy section of marshland looked much like another, in the dark – even if you were a witch.

Well, OK, apprentice witch. Five years of study successfully completed and very nearly graduated. Just the final wild magic practical to complete – the time-honoured ritual that, in its current form, involved the apprentices being dropped off by minibus at dusk, somewhere on the island. They then had until dawn to orient themselves and gather the objects required to make their own way back to the Academy by more traditional means.

Although justifiably proud of its ancient heritage, one of the stated aims of the Manx Academy of the Wiccan Arts was to produce versatile witches capable of dealing with the challenges they would face in the 21st century. Consequently, after studying ancient grimoires and learning spells by rote for the first four years of their time at the Academy, final year students were strongly encouraged to explore alternative ingredients and approaches. The practical test specified a broom and flying ointment combination that was traditional for the Isle of Man, but it was rumoured that the examiners awarded extra points for suitable alternatives. Kerry did another mental run through of the list.

'A besom or broom, with the shaft cut by the witch's own hand from hawthorn, correctly trimmed of branches and with birch twig bristles, attached with a willow withy.' Check. Even starting at dusk that bit had been fiddly, but Kerry was pretty handy with a billhook. As for the ingredients for the flying ointment, they'd taken the rest of the night.

'The grease of a fatted pig.' Kerry was vegetarian, so that just wasn't happening, but lanolin worked just fine. Of course, they'd been allowed to prepare the base in advance and bring it with them, which was just as well, because obtaining grease from either sheep's wool or an unfortunate pig was a task that would take even an expert witch more than a few hours.

'Wraick from the seashore, gathered from below the tide line but at the height of the tide.' Check. The still damp denim flapping around Kerry's legs was a testament to that. That updated drying spell using chili powder was pretty effective, though.

'Copper from the heart of the Earth to anchor the witch.' Check. Fortunately the Isle of Man had been a major mining centre in its day, and if you knew where to look you could find remnants of lots of different metal ores. The minibus had deposited Kerry on Laxey promenade, opposite the chip shop, and it had been a slog walking up from the seashore past the giant water wheel to the former mines and over the hills. Kerry was once again thankful that the island was relatively compact. It must be a sod having to do this practical somewhere bigger.

Although, again, you learned the magic that was fitting for your environment. In the fourth year, they'd done a study visit to London and seen some of the urban resources their peers were learning to use; pigeon shit rather than seagull or sheep, rose bay willow herb and other plants of waste ground, plenty of stuff about 'foul steaming breath' – in other words, car exhaust...and Kerry had been fascinated to discover the power contained in the superimposed layers of fly posters, if selected from the right spot.

'Water hemlock to lift her from the soil.' Yeah, well that was the problem, wasn't it?

An owl hooted close by, and Kerry jumped. "Lacks concentration" had been a frequent criticism from the Academy's tutors, and especially from Mistress Voirrey, one of the self-proclaimed 'Modern Witches' amongst their number, yet who had nevertheless opposed Kerry's presence, from admission onwards. But as the best Manx-born talent the Academy's interviewers had seen for many years, Kerry couldn't be denied a place.

Kerry sighed again and peered through the gloom. Now where had this blasted water hemlock got to?

*OK, think clearly. We came in from the front of the Wildlife Park, and skirted around the enclosures, and it was somewhere near the back of the lake that I saw the hemlock. Today I've come in from the seaward side...*Kerry squinted up at the line of the hills above, with the outline of Gob y Volley visible against the Milky Way.

...so if I go over this way, then I should find the fence pretty quickly and then from there it'll be easy as...well, easy as smashing all the ingredients up on a stone with my pestle, mixing them with the pot of lanolin, and rubbing it on to the broomstick. A quick flight back to Slieu Whallian – ideally resisting the urge to do a victory roll over the Principal's garden this time, given the trouble it got me in last year – and even a tolerably tidy landing will have me in the history books...

But once again, Kerry hadn't been paying attention. In the dark, the tall wire fence around the Wildlife Park was almost totally invisible. The outermost, electrified fence was completely so. The current running through it was low – just a deterrent to keep animals, both native and exotic, on their respective sides of the boundary – but it still gave off a nasty shock. Kerry leaped backwards onto the soft ground, twisting frantically to avoid falling onto the pot of lanolin...and heard a resonant "Crack" as the shaft of the broomstick snapped.

'Dammit.' Kerry examined the damage. It was a clean break, right through, and the bristles weren't looking too clever either. Finding another straight trunk of hawthorn down here in the Curraghs was going to take hours. And there wasn't much time left. The sky in the east was definitely beginning to get lighter.

Although at least the water hemlock problem was finally solved, because Kerry was surrounded by the stuff. It was growing in thick clumps along the ditch at the base of the fence. Dragging on a pair of rubber gloves as she remembered Mistress Onnee's cheerful words of warning – "Never mind a black cat! A nice pair of Marigolds are a witch's best friend!," Kerry bent carefully beneath the electrified wire and collected a good handful of the toxic plant, frantically wondering all the while what to do next. The broomstick was a no go, that much was clear. *What else, what else? Think, brain!*

Coming to stillness and breathing deeply, as Mistress Joaney had advised in Basic Meditation for Spellcasters, Kerry strove for a calm mind and an open spirit. What had they been taught on the London trip about suitable objects for flight? There had been something, something…

But an insistent noise kept impinging – a kind of scritching noise, like nails on the blackboard. It was familiar yet alien at the same time. It reminded Kerry of hot sunshine and the taste of melted ice cream in a soggy cornet. It was the sound of a summer holiday coach trip. It was the smell of the reptile house and the okapi enclosure. It was the sound…of a group of large sleepy birds expressing their discontent with the early morning chill.

Kerry suddenly grinned broadly. That elusive phrase spoken by the London instructor suddenly resurfaced. "Don't forget. In a pinch you can use pretty much anything as a broomstick, providing it's roughly the right shape. Something that has the life force in it is best, but failing that a lamppost or traffic sign, a patio heater..."

"A garden parasol", Mistress Voirrey had interrupted. "Never forget, ladies..." She'd scowled at Kerry before continuing, "...never forget that as modern witches, we aren't limited by traditional beliefs or components. You will always be taught the traditional methods first, but you may elaborate upon these with new materials, if they can be made to work according to the Rules of Witchcraft."

So...an alternative broomstick-shaped object, ideally with the life force in it? Yes. And there'd be no need for the water hemlock, after all. The object Kerry had in mind didn't merely have the life force in – it could fly too, in its natural form at least. So a simple element to cancel her own weight, such as dandelion or thistledown, would do the trick.

The whole thing was definitely doable, providing she could scale the fence. Fortunately, she'd been a terrible tearaway when she was a little boy, and it wouldn't be the first time she'd broken into somewhere. The only problem with the entire plan was that Mistress Voirrey was probably going to have kittens at the sight of the Academy's first transgender student landing on the West Lawn on a bright pink flamingo...

Making Friends

She's slumped in the sweltering shade in the garden, sweating and irritated, when she first hears the noise. Of course, that's not actually strictly true – she was a kid when she first heard it in some corny old film, and there was one on that Bowie track. But this is the first time she's ever heard the sound in real life.

It doesn't register to begin with. There are cars driving past in the distance, and she's just so hot that nothing's really sinking in.

Then she thinks it might be a notification on her phone, some new app that makes a noise like... And that's when she sees it. It's gliding down in the middle of the lawn, about 50 metres away. She knows what it is immediately, even as she's walking, disbelieving, towards it – a pterodactyl. Smallish, maybe 50 cm from one wingtip to the other. As she gets closer, she can see that it's definitely artificial, but at the same time kind of...organic? Covered in dark brown stuff that looks like velvet or the short fur on a cat's ear. It looks up at her from where it's crouching awkwardly on the parched grass and goes "Squeeeeee?"

She can't stop herself calling it Terry. It has a little crest on its beak, but not a very obvious one, so she can't work out if it's meant to be any specific gender.

She discovers that these days they aren't called pterodactyls any more, but pterosaurs. And that in fact they aren't even dinosaurs.

She never finds out where it came from. Nobody seems to be missing a robot dinosaur. Or if they are, they aren't looking for it very hard.

She goes on a date with Johan, a guy she doesn't really find attractive, just because his profile mentions that he's a palaeontologist. They actually have quite a nice time, although there's no way she's going to invite him home.

Terry's a pretty good houseguest. It seems to run on solar power, because it likes to spend a good amount of the day standing about in the sun with its wings partly open like a drying umbrella. The rest of the time it sits on her desk in a cardboard box filled with tissue paper, which it tears up periodically with its pointed beak, dropping the bits onto her desk as if bringing her gifts. It doesn't ever eat anything, although it occasionally snaps at flies if they're bothering her, which is endearing but kind of scary because it's so quick. It catches them quite often, too, dropping the squashed remains on the little heap of paper beside the box. At night it insists on clambering up the stairs with her when she goes to bed, where it sleeps on her discarded clothes.

It smells of cinnamon and gun oil, and now so does she. Several people are complimentary about her new perfume.

Terry's pretty ungainly on the ground, because its wings don't really fold up tidily, and it has to walk like a bat, kind of on its elbows. But it can launch itself into the air by doing a surprisingly high leap off all fours, and once there it's really quite nippy. They play frisbee in the garden, her throwing and Terry snapping the plastic disc out of the air and dropping it at her feet.

As the weather finally gets cooler, she notices that Terry's moving more slowly, so she brings out the big daylight lamp and the robot pterosaur does its umbrella trick in front of that instead.

After it's been with her about six months, Terry occasionally starts coming over and pecking at her keyboard, then peering at the screen. She shows it how to type "Terry," though it doesn't seem to understand. But a few weeks later she comes downstairs in the morning and discovers that she's apparently ordered a whole load of electronic components from Kjell & Company, plus some stuff she can't even identify from a lab equipment supplier. When she confronts Terry with the email confirmations, it gives a tiny pterosaur shrug and settles down in its box.

The deliveries start arriving a few days later. She feels ridiculous trudging up to the village shop in the snow to collect packages ordered by a pterosaur, but she does it anyway, bringing them back and laying them out on the garage floor. Terry shuffles up and down, inspecting the items and turning them over with its beak. She digs out her old laptop and sets that up on the floor too, and watches as the robot pterosaur taps away at the keys, occasionally using a rear claw or a forelimb to move the mouse.

It clearly understands English, but it never communicates with her directly other than with the odd squawk or crooning noise that a cat might make to its human. She wonders if it somehow can't associate the sounds she makes with the symbols it sees on the screen.

At any rate, after a day or two using a freeware CAD program, it produces a neat diagram showing how all the parts fit together. She's pretty good with a soldering iron, and she's used to making models for wargaming, so it kind of makes sense. She prints out the diagram, lays out the tools she thinks she's going to need, and starts work, with Terry watching closely.

It takes her nearly a month, because some of the organic parts have to be grown in glass beakers. They just look like blobs to her, but sure enough when she lays the blobs in the right place in the structure, they ooze into position like they've always been there.

And when she's finished, Terry squawks in satisfaction and stabs at the Enter key on the laptop, and the second pterosaur – a bit chunkier, a bit more obviously robotic – looks up at her from where it's crouching awkwardly on the garage floor and goes "Squeeeeee?"

Behind You

It amuses me to observe her as she observes others. She sits in the centre of the café, so absorbed in noting down the traits of the people in her line of sight that she doesn't think to look behind her, where she would instantly spot me, watching her every gesture and smiling.

She is young, this girl, no more than early 20s, and the fresh curve of her cheek and the eager way she bends over her tatty notebook with each new inspiration remind me of myself at that age.

She has skin the colour of milky coffee, smooth black hair tied back into a short, neat pony tail and wears clothing that seems somehow too thin for the season. But perhaps she is one of those trusting souls who leave their coats on the rack beside the door. I've never been able to, myself. This is London, after all, not some village in rural...what is she, Indian? Thai, perhaps? I can just make out that the characters she is so diligently scribbling in her notebook are not English. But she's most likely a local, like me – as far as anyone is ever local in London – and simply confident in her youth.

I find myself wondering whether, in another 20 years, I will be even more cynical and defensive than today. And I look over my shoulder, just in case that older me is already there, making notes.

Guardian Angel

Once upon a time in a land not so very far away there lived a very spoiled little girl called Lucy. Golden of hair and blue of eye she was, and as fair as the bright morning sunshine, but her heart was as grey as granite, and much harder.

For she was an only child, and her parents owned a big house with a fine park and thought themselves better than all the folk around. And they gave their Lucy such airs and graces that no other child would have anything to do with her, for they'd no sooner show Lucy their favourite toy than she'd snatch it away from them or break it or have a screaming fit and say the other child had pinched her or pulled her shining hair.

And so, although she was a very spoiled little girl and had everything she could want in the way of material goods, she had no friends – no, nor even any way to know what it was she was missing when she felt their lack.

Instead of real flesh-and-blood children to be her friends, Lucy had to content herself with made-up friends. With princesses and kings and rulers of far-off lands who just happened to be strolling in her father's grounds when she took her daily walk. But as I'm sure you know, an imaginary friend is all very well for conversation and how-de-do, and what a fine dress you have there, but not much use when it comes to giving you a boost up a tree so you can sit in the branches with a book and an apple.

Aye, pretty and rich she might be, but Lucy was probably the loneliest lass in the whole land in those days.

So you can imagine her delight when, one bright and breezy day, as she took her solitary walk through the parkland of her father's estate, she came across a splendidly dressed being, standing quietly by the ornamental fountain where she was wont to loiter for many a long hour, amusing herself by playing with the cool water and admiring how the jets of liquid sparkled in the sunlight.

The figure was tall and upright and dressed all in golden robes. Lucy couldn't say if it was man or woman, and when it shook itself a little and straightened still more at her approach, she realised to her astonishment that the figure had two neatly pleated golden wings on its back.

"G..good day," she stammered, for even proud young girls are apt to be a little taken aback when encountering an angel.

"Good day, Lucy," replied the figure gravely, inclining its head, but making no other move or comment.

"Ah... Perhaps you would like to come into the house, to meet Mama and Papa?" asked Lucy nervously.

"Thank you, not just now," said the angel. "I am a guardian angel and I have a duty to remain here for the moment."

Lucy became even more nervous, looking wildly around. Her parents had often implored her to take a servant with her while walking in the grounds, but she had thrown such tantrums at the thought of having to be accompanied by a person of low rank that they had stopped suggesting it. And the sad truth is that Lucy was such unpleasant company that neither her father nor her mother considered walking with her themselves.

Lucy knew nothing of this, of course. But she feared that her parents' dire predictions of bandits and ne'er-do-wells trying to steal her fine gold necklace or pearl brooch had come true. However, she could see no one amongst the tended lawns and hedges of the garden. The only movement came from the trees and shrubs waving their branches in the strengthening breeze.

"Are you here to save me?" she demanded. "From what, pray? Ugh!" For a large greenish-black beetle had fallen from the pine tree above the fountain and landed in her hair. Feeling it moving amongst her golden curls, Lucy shrieked loudly and flailed at it, shaking her head and calling out to the angel, "Get it off! Get it off!"

But the angel did not move, simply watched her actions until, finally, with a shudder of disgust, she dashed the insect from her hair, sweeping it into the basin of the fountain, where it lay struggling in the water.

"Will you not save it from drowning?" asked the angel calmly.

"Indeed I shall not!" snapped Lucy, stamping her foot. "The horrid thing was in my hair. I shall have to ask Nanny to wash it now that nasty creature has touched it."

"Indeed?" enquired the angel mildly. "But the beetle will die if you do not help it."

"Good!" retorted Lucy huffily. "I'm going back to the house. Are you coming?"

"I have a duty to remain here, for the moment."

"I don't see how you can guard me from here if I'm in the house," said Lucy rudely. "I don't believe you're a guardian angel at all." And with that, she swished her cloak and her golden hair and set off indignantly back along the grassy path to the house.

But she hadn't taken more than a few steps when a branch from the pine tree – weakened by the beetle attack and the force of the wind – crashed down from above and killed her dead.

If she had but taken the few seconds to rescue the beetle from the water, she would have been quite unscathed.

The angel sighed, and dipped one finger into the water, allowing the beetle to climb thankfully onto its golden skin.

"I *am* a guardian angel," the angel said with quiet emphasis. "I just didn't say whose." And the angel watched, as the beetle, now completely dry, flew away into the bright, breezy day.

Twenty Four Twelve Twenty

We still hear other voices, sometimes. Voices in the darkness, through the crackling static and the whine of the radio waves.

Men's voices, mostly. There don't seem to be so many women – and I look around our small group which is mostly women now and I wonder, does that mean our group is different to have so many? Or do the women in those other camps out there, those audio sparks in the dark night...do they just save their energy for more practical things than keeping in touch with what's left of the human race?

I know some of the voices now as I didn't when I was younger. The Tingler, from somewhere in central Europe. Sanna, from Norway, who just sings and cries now although I remember when she used to speak. Omar, who speaks Arabic so all we can understand is his name. Years ago it seemed normal to me that there were people talking, singing or swearing from the radio set in the corner of the big house. And there seemed to be so many of them, overlapping and competing with each other, sharing their news. Some of them even having conversations, lucky in being able to transmit and receive, where we have only ever been able to listen.

Now there are fewer voices, and they've settled into a routine, I suppose a bit like the radio programmes Mara told us kids about during our school time. That was when we still had school time. When there were enough children to make it worth an adult spending time on teaching us about how the world used to be.

I was sick when the other kids left, a year ago. I'd been sick for a few days, so I didn't even hear them talking about it, but I can guess who started it. Lee was always the leader of our little gang, always the one urging us to do things we shouldn't or that we didn't really know how to do. Like trying to blow up the rusting car in the corner of the top field – which didn't blow up but made a huge cloud of thick black nasty smelling smoke – or making magic potions out of the bright coloured liquids on the top shelf of the workshop cupboard, which put Anna in the sickbay for a week and the rest of us on hard chores for a whole month.

So when the other children escaped... I knew it was because of Lee. Recently he'd been saying he thought the leaders were just keeping us in the compound because they were stupid, or mad, or sick or something. His reasons seemed to change every day, with each new kid he explained his theory to.

"It's because most of them are girls", he'd said to me scornfully. "Girls are always scared of everything. The leaders have been out and seen the world and all the big machines and roads and other people out there and they're scared and they don't want us to go out because then they'll have to as well, and we'll see the world is just like it always was. There's just us stuck in here, in this stupid compound."

"But the radio..." I protested.

"Fake!" he screeched. "All fake, made up by the government to keep us in our place."

"But..." In the face of such certainty I was beginning to doubt what Mara had taught us, the books we'd read. "But...we've been out", I finally stammered. "We've seen what it's like out there, the roads all smashed and the broken cars everywhere and all the towns burned or in ruins."

Last winter Lee and I were both 11 and the oldest of the kids. And so we were allowed to start going out on patrols with the adults, trying to salvage anything useful that hadn't already been looted loads before. One time we walked for five days away from the compound and still didn't see another living human. There must've been some around, because we came across a car that was still burning, but there was no driver at the wheel and no sign of where one might have gone.

But even so, I couldn't see how Lee could possibly think this was all some kind of hoax. What would be the point? We weren't that important. Why would anyone ruin so much of the country just to keep the 40 of us in our little compound?

Lee was stubborn, though, and the other kids were in awe of how he stood up to the adults, and so when it turned out one December morning that all the kids were gone – at least all of them older than four-year-old Fiona – well, I hadn't exactly been expecting them to do something so stupid or I'd have warned Samira or Joanna, but I wasn't entirely astonished either. I was surprised we never got them back, though. I expected them to be gone for hours at most. But we'd all been taught how to operate the motorbike, and they'd taken it and the bike trailer too, so they had a good head start. And it began snowing that morning, heavy fat flakes drifting down like feathers, the thickest snow any of us had ever seen, even Joanna, and she's ancient. So by the time we worked out they'd headed east, towards what was once a big city called Birmingham (I can't really imagine a city, but Mara used to tell us about them, and there's a picture of a place called Liverpool in one of our books)... Well, anyway, the roads were blocked and the search party couldn't get through. And Samira just said she'd never send more of our people there, not after... And then she looked at me and Fiona and stopped speaking and the adults went and argued in the workshop for a long time. In the end, Louise and Diane went after their three kids, and Brendan went with them – still insisting Lee couldn't have been involved and that it was all a government conspiracy. And Eddie and Richard went as well, but they left their wives behind. Only after a week Marie and Sara went away one night too. So now there are only 24 of us.

None of them came back. Nobody who ever goes east ever comes back. Sometimes, when I was little, walkers would come to the compound, in ones and twos – ragged, tired-looking people. We'd swap food for information, and one of them was James and he stayed, but none of the rest of them seemed to be much use and so we didn't let them in and after a day or two they'd move on. And we'd never see them again.

So I listen to the voices on the radio, at night – always at night, they're strongest then – and I dream of where those voices are coming from. I've been thinking that we'd get a better signal if we had a bigger antenna. I reckon I could climb out of the attic window of the big house at night, onto the roof, where the antenna's attached to the chimney, and fasten it to a scaffolding pole instead – I know where there is one in the long grass behind the workshop – and then I could attach the pole to the chimney and that would make the antenna loads taller, and that would be a great Christmas present for everyone and cheer them up from thinking about last year. I'll be careful though – I'm going to tie myself to one of the steel brackets. I've got lots of rope.

Conveying the Purple Frog

"Ready?"

"Ready." Helen shifted in her uncomfortable chair, shut her eyes and tried to relax. She really wasn't in the mood for this today.

"OK," came Tom's voice from inside the house. "I'm visualising an object. I'm holding it in my hand, and looking at it carefully, viewing it from every angle. I'm smelling it..." He paused. "And touching it with my fingertips, feeling the texture..."

She loved to listen to his voice. When they first met, three years earlier at a meeting of the Psychics' Society, she'd been attracted to his warm, velvety tones from the start, and she had never tired of hearing him speak.

Concentrate! she thought to herself. *This is important!* She wriggled her shoulders and tried to tune in properly.

The ESP technique they had developed together was revolutionary, and the result of three years' intensive trial and error. The result, too, ultimately, of that first meeting in a freezing cold church hall one February night, after which they had gone to the pub to defrost with the other attendees from the meeting

– and never really been apart since. Her friends at work had thought she was mad even to go to the meeting in the first place.

"A load of loonies," Lisa had said, picking the currants out of her hot cross bun, when Helen had mentioned that she intended to go. "You'll end up in a pork pie, my girl, and if you do don't come running to me!"

"She's right," Mandy had agreed, adjusting her headset over her new hairdo for the umpteenth time that morning. "Ghosts and ESP and all that. A load of effing... Accounts department, Mandy speaking, how may I help you?"

Helen had laughed and shrugged off their comments. She'd just had a feeling she ought to go to the meeting, the instant she'd seen it advertised in the local paper. She'd always had an uncanny aptitude for card games, and she'd read somewhere that this could indicate someone with a high natural level of ESP.

And she'd been right. She and Tom had a connection the first time they set eyes on each other. Not exactly love at first sight, but definitely something special. And now they were really starting to get somewhere. Tom had recorded the latest version of their specially designed instructions, and now she listened to the recording every night as she slept. By combining this sleep study with hearing him *sending* the object, using equally carefully developed wording, they'd achieved amazing breakthroughs.

Before each session, Tom would go into town without her and scour the charity shops for suitable objects. They needed things that were a uniform colour and relatively simple in shape – and above all that Helen hadn't already seen or touched. They were kept in a large cardboard box in the corner of the study, which she was under strict instructions not to open.

Last time they'd done really well. She'd got the bright pink colour of the jug and the shiny surface of the mirror. Maybe this time she'd get the object itself. If only she could concentrate.

"Anything?" said Tom, appearing in the open patio door behind her.

She turned and smiled ruefully at him.

"Afraid not," she said. "But we've only just started. Let's try the next one."

"Right oh," he said cheerfully, disappearing back into the house, then popping his head out again.

"Oh, by the way, that one was a big yellow chrysanthemum."

A yellow chrysanthemum? She'd had no feeling of yellow, or any idea that the object had been a flower. She sighed and shifted again in her chair. Last time they'd tried this it hadn't been so sunny. Maybe that was making a difference. Or maybe it was the sight of Rascal, their tiny Yorkshire terrier, sniffing about the garden. Resolutely, she shut her eyes again.

"Ready," she called.

"Right. I'm visualising an object..."

But today nothing worked. She kept getting distracted by Rascal's antics, by the smell of the flowers, the noise of nearby weekend lawnmowers and the swallows darting above the house. They tried for two hours, until she was exhausted from 'listening' and Tom was hoarse. Although their best results had previously been achieved with her on the veranda and him indoors, they tried it with her indoors, in the same room as Tom; even back to back. But nothing appeared.

The ring with the red stone, the blue ball, the purple plastic frog...all the objects Tom visualised remained stubbornly invisible to her. Eventually they gave up for the day.

"Never mind," said Tom into her hair as he gave her a consolatory hug. "We did really well last week and we can't expect to make progress every time." He stepped back and slapped his hands together.

"Now let's take Rascal out for a walk and blow the cobwebs away. And then this evening maybe we could have a pizza and go to the pictures, what do you think?"

She hugged him back. She loved him so much. And she knew that one day he'd be famous – they both would – for having achieved success with their new method. It would just take more time, that was all.

As he trotted in front of them along the path to the common, Rascal decided that his favourite had been the blue ball. Although the purple frog had looked interesting too.

The Fate of Circumstances

She was at school the first time she read Thomas Hardy's poems – set texts for her O-levels that she was surprised to enjoy.

Soon after that she started going out with her first real boyfriend. It lasted, on and off, until he failed his A-levels – she was never sure why, as he didn't seem to struggle in class – and she went off to university. She met a guy called Andy in the first term, and never looked back.

She was living in rural Scotland with Andy, the second time she read Thomas Hardy's poems. She just spotted a copy in the local library and felt again that same feeling of gentle excitement and comprehension as she flicked through the pages.

Soon after that, she fell in love with a client, astonishingly, over a meeting table. She couldn't take her eyes off him, and he kept looking up and seeking her gaze with a tiny, shy stunned smile of his own. After the meeting, they both just walked away in the same direction, ending up in a cafe and talking for hours. This was Jon.

Ten years later, Jon left her for a younger woman, a woman who would give him the children he so desired. "I still love you, but..." as he put it. She'd told him right from the start, in that cafe, that she didn't want kids, but couldn't feel angry that he'd changed his mind.

She'd been living happily on her own for four years the third time she read Thomas Hardy's poems. They'd slipped from her consciousness again, but one day something made her think of them. And by now she had enough money that she could afford to buy an attractive, cloth-bound copy of Wessex Poems. These were mostly new to her, but still with that same spare style and lucidity. She just got him, his references and his thinking. Funny to share your character with a Victorian Romantic. Or maybe not.

Three weeks later, she got a message through her shortest and least impressive dating profile, from a man who described himself as "Not really looking for anyone at the moment but I just had to contact you." His profile was the longest and most impressive one she'd ever seen. She was visiting his town two days later and suggested coffee, knowing that he almost certainly wouldn't be able to make it. He could. They hugged when they first met, and she felt like she'd come home.

Scanning her bookcase later that week, not really knowing what could possibly entertain her mind through the jittery love-struck haze engulfing her, she spotted Wessex Poems. Reached slowly towards the small volume and drew it out carefully, opened it and flicked through it, wondering.

Then she smiled sadly and replaced it gently, for the next time.

In Space, No One Can Hear You Whisk

Noémie was halfway through preparing the kirsch and chocolate ganache for her signature bake – a gooey multi-layered chocolate cake, loosely based on a Black Forest gateau – when she remembered Mac's message again and started welling up.

"The bastard," she reminded herself, channelling the anger and hurt into her spatula. The absolute bastard. How could he choose now, when she was up to her ears in chocolate and sequestered in an exclusive living unit at the other end of the habitat – and being filmed all day right across the weekend, too – to tell her he was leaving her?

And why? It wasn't as though they'd been getting on badly. In fact he'd been really supportive since she'd qualified for Bake Off, helping her work out her recipes, endlessly testing the different versions and really taking an interest.

She tasted the ganache with a teaspoon. Perfect. She hadn't put quite as much kirsch in it as Mac liked, but she thought it was more balanced like this. Anyway, sod him, she thought, ramming the mixture into a piping bag with slightly more force than was really necessary. How bloody dare he?

He knew that winning the GSBO was Noémie's dearest dream, and that she'd thought and talked of almost nothing else since she'd heard Isolde habitat was going to get its own show.

Not that Izzy didn't deserve it, she thought proudly, looking briefly out of the clear plastic sides of the tent at the parkland around – and beyond that at the landscape curving up in both directions in the distance.

When she wasn't piping flawless spirals of chocolate ganache onto deliciously light sponge cake, she loved to explore the hidden, backstage areas of the habitat as part of the human maintenance team. Their efforts weren't strictly necessary, of course – Izzy was completely self-maintaining – but there were always tasks that it was easier for a human to do, like those requiring climbing, strength *and* manual dexterity, which was a fiddly combination for Izzy's bots to achieve. So Noémie spent some of her time dressed in red overalls, squeezed into tight spaces or up ladders, wrestling with stuck bolts or shattered seals. She enjoyed it, the mixture of physical and mental, the insight into what was involved in keeping her home secure and comfortable. Mac had never understood that, either.

She put the piping bag down and straightened, rubbing her aching back. Yes, it was perfect. She gently lifted the next slender disk of chocolate sponge, taking care to support it in the centre to prevent it breaking, and placed it on top of the ganache. The cake was taking shape nicely now, and if she could just stay focused she'd be fine.

Although she still couldn't quite believe she was here, *in the tent!* She'd always wanted to be here, from the first moment she saw the 150th anniversary series as a little girl. There had been clips from all sorts of Bake Offs. The original series, filmed in what had then been the UK, and which laid down the rules and format for all Bake Off competitions ever since; the first Luna colony competition, where the tent had been pressurised and the competitors had done their walk across an artificial green lawn in space suits, entering the tent through an airlock; images of the worst disasters and the greatest feats. Noémie's favourite had been the multi-coloured sugar angel made on Phobos in season 63. But she'd always tried to avoid thinking about the failures. The collapsed sculptures, the burnt offerings – the disasters, when competitors had completely lost it and ended up throwing their creations in the bin, storming out, and on one memorable occasion (*Koko Suomi leipoo*, season 117) trying to drown themselves in the lake. Although she had watched and rewatched the episode in which one competitor had thrown away nine batches of macaroons but had still gone on to win the technical challenge with a fabulous floral garden of delicately coloured gems of the patissier's art. The woman had been French, of course. Noémie was proud to be an Isoldean, but probably even more proud to have French ancestry. The French had practically invented baking, after all.

She stepped back and regarded her cake critically. This was another point over which she and Mac had argued. He'd asserted that the entire cake should be covered in chocolate buttercream, piped into rosettes and topped with chocolate shavings. But she'd always thought it made the overall result rather sickly, though she had to admit it often looked impressive. She reached reluctantly for a fresh piping bag. Then his message popped into her head again.

She'd received it an hour before they were due to start recording for the day. She'd assumed Mac would be wishing her good luck for this round of the competition, but instead he'd brusquely said that he didn't feel the relationship was going anywhere and that he'd asked Izzy to assign him new quarters. He'd be gone when she got back after this session of the filming, he said. And because he'd chosen to send it as a dead clip rather than a live conversation, she hadn't even had the chance to ask why he'd suddenly made such a decision. She'd tried to message him back, of course, but Izzy's sweet tones had informed her that Mac had blocked her as a sender. She couldn't understand it. Yes, things had been a bit rocky for a while, but ever since the first pre-series session, where all the competitors and their families had been invited to a 'get to know you' evening, she'd thought things were better. He really had devoted a lot of time to her entries for each round, and although they still hadn't been having much sex – well, none at all, actually – she'd really thought they were doing OK again. But apparently not.

Well, sod him, she thought again. She had plenty of time, and judging by the muttered cursing coming from behind her, Selina, her closest rival, was struggling with her own creation. She'd abandon impressive and go for elegant instead: dark chocolate mirror icing with a hint of orange. And she'd add some swirly chocolate decorations and a spot of gold leaf, too. Now, where was that tempering thermometer?

She won the signature challenge. The judges said they'd have liked more kirsch flavour, but her Black Forest gateau looked fabulous and had plenty of cherries in. She'd noticed in earlier rounds that one of the judges, Gareth Chu – Isolde's best patissier and the driving force behind the arrival of Bake Off on the habitat in the first place – was particularly keen that cakes with fruit in should be liberally filled with whatever those fruit were.

She also thanked her lucky stars – or perhaps more her own taste buds – that she'd abandoned Mac's preference for buttercream and instead gone for the mirror icing, which was praised for being 'elegant and with just the right balance of sharpness'. Poor Selina's offering, a family recipe involving hazelnuts, caramel, milk chocolate and raspberries, had looked like it had been thrown together in five minutes – probably because it had, Selina being a bit of a dreamer and not great at managing her time in the tent – and received the ultimate insult of being described as 'too sweet'.

Noémie had felt sorry for the other woman. She and Selina had grown quite close since the start of the competition. Mac and Noémie had even met up with Selina for a drink one evening when neither of the women were practicing their bakes. Though Selina's wife had apparently been unable to make the encounter. "She's just not awfully sociable," Selina had explained, but Noémie had got the idea that all was not well between them.

The three of them had a good time together anyway, in a new bar that Izzy had just created. This one was threaded like a huge diamond bead on a sparkling rod of water-filled crystal, spanning the habitat's internal space. The crystal rod was open at the top and ran through the centre of the bar like a glowing river of translucent blue, and if you were bold – or drunk – enough, you could throw yourself into its rushing waters and be transported all the way to the rim. Noémie hadn't even considered it, but Selina and Mac had gigglingly dared each other to do it and before she could wonder whether it might be fun after all, Selina had grabbed Mac's hand and they'd run up to the narrow platform bridging the channel and launched themselves into the torrent.

Mac had got back to their quarters several hours later, dry but with a selection of scrapes and bruises. Izzy's safety protocols didn't protect her inhabitants from minor injuries, but Noémie had been surprised by the red raw patches on his knees and elbows, covered in transparent healskin.

"I'm fine, stop fussing," he'd said irritably when she commented upon it. "That tube's a bit turbulent, that's all. It was fun, though." And his eyes had shone.

"Maybe we could do it together sometime?" Noémie had suggested.

"What babe?" said Mac absently. "Oh. No. I don't think it's your kind of thing. Did you see that Selina though? She's fearless, that woman!"

"I know!" exclaimed Noémie. "Did I tell you about her Showstopper last week? I wish you could have seen it. It was fabulous."

Mac smiled at her. "Well I'll see it when the series is screened, won't I?"

Sitting in the makeup room, Noémie tried not to think about how they wouldn't be watching it together, now. Not that she wanted to see herself on screen, but she'd kind of hoped to be looking back at the series from the winner's perspective, reliving all the ups and downs on her path to victory, seeing how she'd finally achieved her greatest ambition – with Mac.

Anyway, now wasn't the time for those thoughts. It was technical challenge time.

She thanked the makeup man and went to join the others in the foyer of the mansion, prior to the walk across to the tent. Selina came up and slipped her arm around Noémie's waist, and they hugged each other for a moment.

"Are you OK?" asked Selina. "I mean with Mac leaving. It can't be easy."

Noémie was startled. He'd only left the day before. Did everyone know? She looked around, but nobody else seemed to be taking any notice. Adrian, the youngest competitor, was entertaining the others with impressions of his new puppy, alternating doleful eyes with playful growling and pretending to pee everywhere. No sympathetic faces were turned her way, nobody was obviously trying not to stare. So maybe only Selina knew? But how did she, even?

Noémie asked her. "Oh," and the other woman looked flustered for a second, but then said, "Izzy told me. I was going to invite you both for a drink next week, but Izzy said, and so..."

Noémie kept her face calm with an effort. "It was a shock," she admitted. "But I can't let it affect my performance, so I'm going to pretend it hasn't happened for now...I'll think about it on Tuesday when we've got through this round."

Selina clapped her hand to her mouth and gulped. "Oh, you're so brave, Noémie," she breathed. "I don't know how you can do it. If Angie had left me right in the middle of Bake Off, I'd be a total mess, I just know I would."

Noémie just smiled, well aware that if she spoke another word she'd start howling, which was what she felt like doing. And Selina wasn't really helping, although she obviously meant well.

Fortunately the film crew started bustling about just then, chivvying them around into position and she had to think about looking suitably relaxed yet determined for the cameras. So she hooked her arm into Adrian's on one side and scatty but brilliant Trisha the textile designer's on the other, and put her best foot forward.

The technical challenge was a complete nightmare. She was glad, really, because it took her mind off Mac – although she could so easily have been distracted from her efforts by his departure.

But she used some of the concentration techniques she'd found useful when working in Izzy's least hospitable areas, cramped into access gangways or stretching full length across hot pipes. And fortunately she'd at least heard of the recipe they were being asked to recreate, even if she'd never made it herself. She'd had half an inkling when she'd seen the spits set up beside each work bench, but hadn't quite been able to remember exactly how they were used.

"Baumkuchen," Debra the presenter said, clasping her hands in apparent delight. And the second judge, Magenta – the Terran cookery writer famous across the entire system for their lavish desserts – had raised their eyebrows at Noémie's groan, smirked and left the tent with Gareth Chu.

Debra had gone on to explain that because of the length of time taken to complete the recipe, they'd be doing a four-hour session that day and another two the next, after the main bake had time to dry out. Of course that actually meant two full days of filming, because every hour shown on screen was at least two – more often three – in reality.

Baumkuchen was a tricky cake to make, requiring the application of many thin layers of batter to form a trunk-like shape on a spit, which was rotated over a heat source; in this case, a two-metre long row of energy cells per competitor. Finished, the cake would be a long hollow cylinder, with the rings of batter giving the cake its German name – tree cake.

But even that delicate process wasn't all they were being asked to do.

Baumkuchen was the cake. Baumkuchen*spitzen* was a variation in which the cake was cut into neat triangles and then dipped in chocolate. And they had to make 300 of them! Each! "All identical," said Debra, with a wicked smile.

Noémie read the recipe again. The actual ingredients weren't that complicated, but the assembly was going to require a calm head and a steady hand – and good time keeping. She glanced at Selina, who was flipping the recipe card over and over as if searching for more instructions, while scribbling with a stylus on a scratchpad. Noémie wondered if she should give her a hint about how the cake was constructed. But no – it was a competition, after all. And Selina only had to look around when the others started assembling their cakes.

One thing she remembered very clearly from the clip she'd seen of a Baumkuchen being made was that it took a long time to prepare and heat the mould the cake was made on. So while all around her came the sound of food processors, she cut a large piece of greaseproof paper and rolled it around the slightly conical mould, then tied it neatly on with the string she found amongst her supplies. Only then did she mix up the batter. And then, while the batter rested, she assembled the spit, attached the mould, set up the energy cells behind it and a trough beneath to catch the excess batter, and switched on the energy cells. Then she began turning the spit with the handle. By the time the greaseproof paper had started to go golden, both arms were aching and she still hadn't worked out how she was going to turn the spit and pour the batter at the same time. That was when she spotted the switch at the base of one of the arms of the spit. She nudged it with her foot, and sure enough the spit began rotating on its own. Magenta was so sneaky! She wondered whether everyone else would spot that they didn't have to turn the spit by hand.

It turned out that several people didn't for quite some time, with predictably messy results – the messiest being those of Selina, who hadn't even thought to put a tray beneath the spit to begin with.

By the time the four hours were up, Noémie was exhausted, dishevelled and dripping with sweat. The tent was so hot that it was a wonder it hadn't melted, and Sam, a burly man who was normally a wrestling teacher, had fainted – twice! – and had spent much of the challenge lying on the soft grass outside the tent, being monitored by Izzy. And surely, Noémie thought, there had never been so much bad language used during an episode of Bake Off. The editor's job was probably going to be nearly as tough as theirs had been.

But on the whole, she was satisfied. Her cake was a bit oval, because at one point she'd had a disastrous batch of batter, which had meant she'd had to turn off the energy cells for 20 minutes and had stupidly turned off the spit too. That had given the whole construction the time to sag slightly, but given the shrieks from the rest of the tent she felt she'd come off lightly.

Tomorrow's task would be to slice the cake up into rounds, and then cut the rounds into uniform triangles and dip them in chocolate. Fiddly, but hopefully not too complicated. Although given that this was Bake Off and anyone could make a mistake, Noémie wasn't counting her chickens – or even her Baumkuchenspitzen – just yet.

She came second in the technical challenge. All that effort, and only second, she thought – but it turned out that Adrian had recently spent several weeks of his free time in *Virtual Cookery 2180* making Baumkuchen, so she couldn't be too disappointed. The really tough bit was having to move on from the stress and fatigue of the Technical Challenge and go straight into the Showstopper. But she was also excited about getting to present her creation in public. Which was just as well, because just before they were about to start filming again, she discovered exactly why Mac had left her.

Subconsciously, of course, she'd already suspected it for a while. But it was a stupid throwaway phrase that finally tipped her off to what was actually going on.

They were all sitting in the green room, and Trisha mentioned she'd heard Magenta might be planning to leave the show after the current season. Amidst a chorus of protests and denials, Noémie distinctly heard Selina say to Adrian, "Oh, well, you can't trust everything you hear. A rumour can run all over Isolde before the truth has its boots on." Adrian's reaction was lost in the continuing babble, for which Noémie was grateful. Because she'd only ever heard that stupid phrase used by one person before. Mac.

Instantly, it all fell into place – Mac's sudden enthusiasm for helping her perfect her recipes, after being indifferent to her entering the competition right from the start; the timing of his decision to leave her; the fact that Selina's partner could ostensibly never make it to any of the social events they'd been at, not even – and here Noémie groaned aloud at her naivety – to the pre-filming friends and family party. *Everyone* had been there, even both of Sam's husbands, who were something high up in Isolde's management committee. And all those sympathetic comments from Selina about how upset she must be over the split...

Ugh. She felt so stupid. But she also felt relieved, because it all suddenly made sense. And, she realised, she hadn't actually liked Selina much. That 'all girls together' stuff had never felt genuine. Noémie had other non-male friends – real ones – and with them she genuinely felt supported and at ease. She'd never felt that from Selina. Now she knew why.

But a production assistant was ushering them all back into the foyer of the mansion and towards the tent. So once again she'd have to gather her senses and concentrate on her baking rather than her love life. She wondered momentarily if she could maintain the facade while there was so much turmoil going on inside her. But then she saw Selina, coming towards her with a sweet smile – '*too* sweet', Noémie thought, and grinned to herself. She could do this. She could more than do this. If working on Isolde's entrails had taught her anything, it was that she could do impossible things. So she leaped up from her chair and threw her arms around Selina, hugging her and crying "I'm so glad you're here with me! And I'm *sure* you'll do better in this round!" She could tell Selina was a little taken aback at this 'encouragement', so she linked arms with her and continued happily prattling along the same lines as they were filmed walking across to the tent – twice, because the first time Adrian tripped over his own feet in his nervousness.

And then the Showstopper round began.

The signature bake had been reassuringly familiar, and she'd been buoyed up by the novelty of the situation. And the technical bake had been so tough she hadn't really had time to think. But as well as having set herself a fiendishly difficult challenge when she chose her presentation method, the Showstopper turned out to be all about Noémie battling her biggest demon – her own lack of confidence. As she created an elaborate chocolate volcano – a ring of chocolate and raspberry cake pierced throughout by twice-baked crepes dentelles acting as lava tubes, and covered in pieces of Rocky Road cake and caramelised hazelnuts – she drew up and mentally overcame a long list of objections to her, Noémie, as a person, her value as a partner and her ability as a baker.

Ironically, the complexity of her mental battle seemed to smooth the ground entirely for her baking struggle, and all the different elements that had seemed so difficult when she'd practiced her bake at home simply fell into place. When Noémie watched this episode weeks later, secure in her position as the final winner of the Bake Off – something she still couldn't believe – she marvelled at how confident she appeared, how utterly serene. And that insight into her own abilities gave her the final confirmation she needed to set up her own baking school, welcoming people from all over the system to Isolde.

The only aspect that was really onerous was creating the tiny detailed replicas of all the Bake Off contestants and the judges out of marzipan and making them all recognisably individual. The unique style and colour of Magenta's hair were particularly tricky, and she wasn't entirely happy with the result. But Magenta was so distinctive that nobody could possibly mistake them for anyone else. She also struggled not to laugh hysterically when Selina messed up her own chocolate ombre cake three times and had to opt for a simpler version that, once again, was described as 'too sweet', a verdict that saw her definitively ejected from the tent. But only after the grand finale of the episode, when Gareth pressed the button with a flourish, and Noémie's perfectly judged raspberry and chocolate 'lava' poured down the sides of her cake and rushed dramatically towards the tiny replica contestants, stopping just before it reached them and leaving the mini figures safe but surrounded by a sea of dark red deliciousness.

All except Selina's little figure, which was, very unfortunately, swamped with lava... and melted into a sad little blob of pink and yellow goo.

"Well darlings," Magenta said wickedly, with their trademark head toss, "Now that's what I *call* Death by Chocolate."

Roses Have Thorns

We know they're coming. Their ships arrived suddenly as lights in the eastern sky, flashes and flares first interpreted as some kind of cosmic interference. Then this morning they'd travelled close enough for us to see properly. Really close, apparently. I don't quite get the distances, but if it was a riot going on in your street you'd be worried about your flowerbeds.

There are two types of ship. The big red ones are spiky and gnarled, anemones in the grip of some spiteful disease. The smaller white ones look smooth and delicate, like a child's paper aeroplane made out of a lace doily.

And they're fighting. For hours, now, they've been fighting. Everything on Earth has stopped, all of us standing outside craning our heads back to see, or watching the live broadcast, mouths open, trying to understand what's going on.

I didn't find out about the battle until I woke up and couldn't get any bars on my phone. On the TV, experts were speculating, saying it might all just be a hoax, trying to explain why all those expensive telescopes hadn't seen anything. Lots of talk about cloaking devices and FTL travel. But you know what it's like; live reporting gets pretty dull when nobody has any idea what's really going on. The presenters came up with the amazingly original names of the Reds and the Whites for the two sides, and someone made a weak joke about the Wars of the Roses, but nobody was laughing, not even the guy who'd said it. When you see these things crippled or destroyed before your eyes, you don't feel like laughing. You just feel small and pathetic and somehow ashamed.

Now it's dark, and I'm standing on the roof of my building along with neighbours I didn't even know I had. It's cold out here, but I'm wrapped in a blanket belonging to a large woman who brought up armfuls of them. Mine smells of dog. And we're drinking, all of us. Tea, mainly – we are British, after all – but there's a fair bit of booze being passed around too. Every time a bottle comes my way, I take a swig. Some of the stuff tastes like it might have been made in people's bathtubs. Or possibly worse places. But I swallow it anyway.

Down in the street – all across the town, really – there's been a fair bit of noise. Screaming, crashing noises, all kinds of alarms and sirens, smashing glass, singing, and lots and lots of shouting. We're not saying much up here, though.

Someone's brought a telly up too, so as well as seeing the dots of light swirling around each other up among the stars, we're getting a close up view.

And the last red ship has just been cut to pieces by a group of the white doily ones.

I suppose they'll be coming here next.

I wonder if they'll be friendly?

Fragments

She leaves her room and walks towards the lift. She is annoyed to see that there are a load of other people – at least four adults and several children – coming from the other direction. She quickens her pace, arriving at the lift before they have turned the corner. The lift doors are just closing. She is too late, really, but it is either this or travel down in a lift full of people and squawling brats. She dives through the doors just as they shut.

Of course this means that the lights have gone out in the lift. She blunders around in the dark for a few seconds before she finds the buttons, then counts up from the bottom, trying to remember how many floors there are below the one she wants. Her fingers move across the large round buttons as the warm darkness pushes in around her. She presses a button, then another. She has to get out of this smothering darkness, and quickly.

When the door opens, she shoots out of the lift without waiting to see what floor she is on. It isn't pitch black at least, but the light here is very subdued, painting everything a weird dark orange colour. She is in a large open space, some kind of circular lobby with several corridors leading off it. In the centre of the space stands a tall, multi-armed dark figure, like a cross between a bare-branched tree and a woman, its lower limbs melting into a wide trunk that blends with the slightly sticky black surface of the floor.

"Kali?" she thinks. "Is that who I mean?"

Around the figure are scattered others, smaller, equally black but rounder, grotesque creatures with flexible, rubbery limbs and wide sharp-toothed grins. As the first of them begins to ooze slowly towards her with a horrible sucking noise, she turns and flees into the nearest corridor.

"Um, this is a statue", she says, struggling to find the right words in the foreign language, "about the lost children. About children who have disappeared, who are...dead." She looks at the other woman to check that she has understood.

Around them, people walk on through the subway, and in her head are images of the 1960s: Audrey Hepburn and Laurence Olivier, Mia Farrow and Robert Redford. The death of Mia Farrow, strung up like a small bird from a lamppost.

She looks at the small empty bronze shoes and the handwritten notes, each describing the pain of loss.

"Yeah, um," she says.

She walks along a pale, dusty track between low stone walls and orchards. The road curves around the orchard and splits, one arm leading up over the ridge, the other down towards the blue sea in the distance beyond dark tree tops. Behind her, below her, she knows, is the village, of honey-coloured stone with its strange half ruined buildings. On another day she would explore them, try to lay claim to one of them and hope for peace for a while before someone noisier, more expansive, came to take it from her.

But today she just walks on, in the shade and the sunlight, towards the sea.

She wants to find a beach where she can stand with her toes in the sparkling water, but there are no beaches visible yet. First she reaches a section where the track runs along the steep, almost vertical shoulder of the hill, sloping away both above and below her and covered with dense low foliage. The sea is a long way beneath, on her right, and the view is dizzying. She sees a point, a little ahead, where the foliage shrinks away from a bald headland, and feels the fear/attraction that she knows will take her right to the edge.

Standing there, with the seagulls turning and calling above and below her, and the wind lifting her hair, she feels alive and powerful. She lifts her arms to the sky and smiles broadly.

And then, in a movement so sudden it feels perfectly natural, the ground beneath her *shrugs*, and she is launched into the air. Her first – only – thought is resignation; how inevitable that she will die in the deep dark water. And then she is falling down past the green solidity of the sloping land, so close but so far out of reach, down, down, to the solid blue-grey mass of the sea.

Perspectives

The instant I saw him I fell in love with him. He was so finely dressed, so handsome. He stood on the deck of the ship as everyone paid homage to his royal position and beauty, and I knew I would never love another.

I followed the ship, hoping to catch another glimpse of my dearest love, and that night a terrible storm arose. The ship was wrecked, and my beloved was nearly drowned, but I rescued him. All through the night I swam with him in my arms, leaving him on the beach near a large temple in the dawn light.

I watched as a girl came from the temple and found him, and how he awoke and believed her his rescuer. I watched and wept as he fell in love with his supposed saviour.

I went back to my home beneath the sea. But I could not forget the handsome Prince nor my love for him, and all my favourite songs became sad and wistful. Surely if we were together he would love me as I loved him?

I asked my grandmother if mortals could live in the kingdom of the sea. But she said it was impossible.

Eventually, in desperation, I visited the Witch of the Sea, and she gave me a potion that would allow me to live on land, although I would never be able to return to the sea. I would have legs, and be able to dance better than any other mortal, but only in exchange for my voice. I would never sing – nor even speak – again. And every step I took would feel like sharp knives beneath my feet. Finally, the Witch warned me, if my Prince married another woman I would die at dawn the next day. But I made the bargain willingly for the chance to be with my beloved.

I swam to the surface, near where my love had his home, and drank the potion. It was agony. I thought I was dying. But my Prince found me at the water's edge, and my joy was overwhelming when I saw his handsome face looking at me tenderly as he carried me to his palace.

Then I was truly happy. Although I could not speak, I demonstrated my ardour in my willingness to dance for him. He loved to see me whirl and leap, and I loved to perform for him, even though at every step I felt like my feet were being cut to ribbons.

I became his favourite and went with him everywhere. Then one day the blow fell. His father wanted him to marry; to marry a princess he had never met but to whom he had been promised all his life. But he declared to me that he would not marry someone he did not love, and that he had only ever loved one woman. I hoped he meant me, but he said that he loved the girl from the temple, the one who – as he thought – had rescued him from the shipwreck.

I comforted myself with the fact that he would never see that woman again. Dedicated to the temple as she was, she would never marry. And so he would always be mine, and surely he would come to love me eventually?

But fate is cruel. The princess arrived for the betrothal feast – and she was the girl from the temple. She had been sent there only to complete her education. I watched him recognise her, and I saw that she returned his love.

Tonight they will be married on a fine ship out at sea, and in the morning I will be nothing but sea foam.

The instant I saw her I fell in love with her. She was so simply dressed, yet so beautiful and graceful. She pulled me from the ravening waves, saving my life yet stealing my heart. Then before I could thank her she was gone, back to the forbidding temple while my father's servants bustled around me, and I had not even been able to thank her.

I tried to discover her name, but the priestesses would give me no information. I spent many days and nights waiting on the beach in case she should come there again, but she did not.

But I did not entirely waste my time – one morning I found a strange girl, dumb and innocent, who had been thrown ashore there as I had been. I carried her back to my home and had her nursed until she recovered. She kept me a kind of company, dancing for me often and preventing my heart from entirely breaking. But I could not forget the exquisite grace of my love; the shape of her cheek, the curve of her arm.

Not long afterwards, my father reminded me of my impending marriage, to the daughter of one of his friends, a woman who I had never met despite having been promised to her all my life. I swore that I would never marry a woman I did not love, but he would not listen, and soon the bride arrived for the start of the celebrations.

Imagine my joy when I beheld my beloved – the girl from the temple! She had been sent there only to complete her education. As I recognised her, I could see from the light in her eyes that she returned my love.

Tonight we will be married on a fine ship out at sea, and in the morning our happiness will be complete.

Sparkly Fairy Robot Powder

The pot said "Sparkly fairy robot powder." Lo couldn't resist.

The robots *were* small and sparkly, but they didn't look like fairies. More like very tiny versions of Buzz Lightyear covered in glitter. And they got everywhere. In the cat's fur, in the Rice Krispies box, in Lo's homework bag. Lo's mother wasn't happy.

"They'll get washed into the sea and kill the fish," she said.

So Lo carefully collected every last tiny robot and put them in a box. Every night Lo sang to the sparkly fairy robot box before going to sleep.

Then one day it sang back.

The Gift of Tongues

The problem with being a translator is that sometimes you accept a job without checking it thoroughly. Of course in *theory* we peruse every word of the document in advance, verifying any tricky term with our many reputable sources and making learned notes in beautiful calligraphy with a fountain pen, possibly accompanied by a studious "Hm," and a delicately wrinkled brow before accepting the project in graceful terms and spending all the time we need to work on it, gliding thoughtfully around our beautiful home and pausing frequently to sip from a china cup of green tea. You can picture billowing muslin curtains and polished wooden floors, if you like.

In practice, I spot the email notification while I'm checking my phone in the Co-op checkout queue and read "Hi Flora! Can you help with this? It's ancient Drovian, and I know you don't like handwritten documents but it's only about 400 words. The client's willing to pay an extra 100€ rush fee if you can deliver tomorrow. Pretty please? Thanks, Nico." And then the checkout operator is "Good morning"ing me and the woman behind is tutting loudly and is waaay closer than 1 metre, and I've just realised the car needs at least one new tyre, so despite my best judgement I think, "How bad can it be?" and I tap out "Yeah, no problem." and press Send.

And so I find myself back at home in my rather grotty little flat above a kebab shop in the high street, staring at a .jpg of what turns out to be not merely handwritten but hand *scrawled* ancient Drovian. On what looks like wrinkly brown paper but could actually, given the Drovians' penchant for unpleasantness, be skin? Maybe even human skin?

"Hm," indeed.

Personally, I blame my father. When I was very little he was an archaeology lecturer at the university a couple of miles away, and the only side effect was a few school holidays spent in very dusty but rather hot countries, getting to help clean the finds. Oh, and not being allowed to watch Time Team ("Three days? No professional archaeologist would even have the site grid laid out in three days. It's ridiculous! Disgraceful!...") Then he and Mum split up and he started going on more and more extreme field trips, culminating when I was 12 in *two whole months* in the mountains in Ashke. It was a country of its own back then, do you remember? Before the earthquake and the plague and the famine? A tiny one, but a country, nonetheless. Anyway, I don't know if you're familiar with the cultural activities open to 12-year-old girls in an uninhabited rural area of Upper Ashke, but suffice it to say that I returned to the UK with a really good grasp of the Drovian writing system and language.

Over the next couple of years I helped Dad with the translation of the writing on some of the stelae he'd discovered during the excavations, but after that I was old enough to refuse to go on his field trips, and Mum's new husband Eric used to take us to Majorca in the school holidays instead. That was when I first got interested in Spanish. Well, that was when I first got interested in Spanish *boys*, but it gradually turned into an interest in the language, and that became a Spanish degree, and now I'm a Spanish translator. And Drovian. In fact, I'm pretty much the only Drovian translator in the world working outside a university history department.

Actually, that's a bit odd, really. How come someone's even got this document? Just from the photo I can see it's old. Dad never found anything on ?paper? If that's what this is. It was all stone tablets and stelae and grave markers. I got to be a dab hand at doing rubbings of the inscriptions. Even now the smell of wax crayons takes me back to kneeling in the gritty dust with a broad-brimmed straw hat tied firmly on my head against the hot sun, taking rubbing after rubbing of the apparently endless incised messages the Drovians left. Most of them amounted to "Mr Important Lived & Died Here," of course, but there were one or two more interesting ones. That's archaeologically interesting, of course. Not, like, "The great big chests full of gold coins and jewels are buried under this one," but "Lord Beynarh slaughtered the Demon Whose Name Shall Not Be Spoken on this site, 17th day of Ytelk 473, banishing him for one thousand years. Fear His coming, oh mortal."

Yeah...I'd forgotten that. That was a weird one, that one. It was only a small stone, like a mini-gravestone, but kind of powerful, somehow. It was made of coarse yellowish rock and had a nasty spidery symbol on it that I *really* didn't like. The kind of thing where, when you turn your back, you're sure you can hear it moving, making a quiet little grindy noise on its stone. Dad got a bit cross at me translating that one, I don't know why. All he'd say was that it "wasn't suitable," whatever that means. After that he didn't ask me to help him any more. After that, he didn't do much of anything, really. Just set off to Ashke as usual over the Easter holidays in the year I turned 15...and disappeared. He never reached the dig site, or so they said. And then two weeks later the earthquake hit, and they had enough to do without trying to track down one lone Englishman. It's 10 years now since he died. I still miss him. I think of going there myself, sometimes, but of course there's no 'there' to go to any more, really. I've seen the satellite photos. That vast sinkhole where there used to be a mountain...? Brrr. Makes my skin crawl.

Anyway...I do like to keep my hand in with Drovian translation when I get the chance. So although this is a horrible quality image and the stuff it's on is giving me the creeps, even just in a photo, I'd better get on with it. It's weird, the way it's laid out too. If I didn't know better, I'd say it was a letter. But Drovian inscriptions are always just memorial stuff and maybe the odd census record. Not letters.

Dammit, isn't that always the way? You sit down to work and you just start getting into your flow and someone rings the doorbell. Normally here they've rung the wrong one and they want Mr van der Struijs on the other side of the kebab shop. But this one was for me. A parcel! It's not my birthday for months, and I haven't ordered anything, and it's *heavy*! How exciting. I'll just finish translating this letter – not that it can be a letter, of course, who'd be writing a letter in ancient Drovian? But anyway, I'd better do that first because Nico needs it back ASAP, and then I can see what mysterious object someone's sent me. I wonder who it's from?

The Inn at the World's End

They reached the Inn at the World's End at dusk, after many days spent painstakingly threading the shifting channels of the Octopus Archipelago. And if it hadn't been for Reyna's insistence – and her warm embrace in his bedroll at night – he'd never have even attempted the journey. He'd just have stuck to his usual route, reaching Capstone, the last fixed town, before heading back east again. People with sense came to the Inn by dirigible. But Reyna had to be different in everything she did – even down to taking him as a lover. His good fortune, with her deep brown skin and eyes so unlike his own washed out grey eyes and pale hair, so he wasn't complaining.

They moored the Spindrift securely to the jetty made of tough berwood logs set into the jumbled shore of the End of the World, and staggered up the path to the Inn, both of them struggling to find their land legs again after so many days afloat.

Jarn stopped and looked back, watching as the Octopus transformed to blue grey then faded into the shadows behind it, and the clouds and sea before him caught pure gold, then orange, coral, scarlet, turquoise, lilac, purple. Water all the way to...well, nothing, the stories went.

It was said that if you sailed west for more than a day, you entered a region where the air became thick as water and the water brittle as glass. And nobody who'd gone beyond that had survived. Or at least had never come back to tell of what they'd found.

So he didn't understand Reyna's fascination with the Inn. She'd first mentioned it the night they met – afterwards, as they'd been lying entwined together in the cabin of the Spindrift, in a town at the eastern end of his normal trading route. She looked lazily around at the fine burnished wood in the flickering light of the candle lantern and said, "So you're from Capstone?" He wondered, first, how she could know that. They'd not spoken so many words, nor in such quiet spaces, that she'd have picked up on his accent. But then he saw where she was looking, at the hook with his jacket thrown over it; his best jacket, the one in fine, blue-dyed calf skin, the one he'd won in the wrestling contest a couple of winters back, with the shield of Capstone stitched to the right shoulder.

"Aye," he said, capturing her hand in his and kissing her fingers again, nearly ready for another bout and wanting to explore her, this strange woman fallen so readily into his arms.

But she wasn't having it, not yet.

"Have you ever been to the Inn?" she asked, and had grown insistent when he tried to answer the question with a simple "No." She wanted – *needed*, almost, it seemed – to go there, and only a journey by water would do. He asked why she couldn't take a dirigible, if she was so set on visiting the place, and she made some vague reference to airsickness that didn't really make sense to him, then countered with, "If there are airships flying over the Octopus, why don't they chart the way for boats?" And he laughed grimly and explained the difference in status between Waterborn and Skyborn and how the latter would have nothing to do with a sea rat like him. And he'd told her of his family, of who his grandfather had been...and somehow by the end of that night he'd pledged to take her there.

The Spindrift had been his father's boat, and his father's father's before that, built to that strong-minded man's design expressly for the shifting waters of the Octopus. She was shallow drafted and strong hulled to deal with the constantly changing channels of the archipelago of floating islands. Islands only kept in check by the Two Sisters, the fierce currents flowing westwards either side of the End of the World.

His grandfather Ferrin had made the Octopus his own, had visited the Inn more than any other ship owner, and had been famous for his ability to navigate the archipelago, bringing out of it the exceedingly rare pearls that grew only there, tangled in the rocky root tendrils of the floating islands. But Stefan, Jarn's father, hadn't inherited Ferrin's instinct for the Octopus's waterways, and even six-year-old Jarn had seen the contempt in the old man's eyes and the shame on his father's broad red face when the subject came up.

And on the day of the old man's burning, Jarn's father had turned from the pyre and vowed that he would never try that route again, and that he'd see his son in hell before he'd let him risk the Spindrift either. So Jarn had never before sailed those treacherous waters, barring the first few passages clearly visible to all from Capstone's highest point.

Now that he had though, now that he'd experienced that dark mass of jostling rock, stunted, scrubby trees and peculiar wildlife at close quarters, he knew he'd come back. At first, they'd worked together, he and Reyna, when it came to the navigation. But gradually it had become apparent that his choices were the right ones. That he'd inherited his grandfather's ability to find his way through the maze, by some means he couldn't even describe except by saying, "That way feels right." So almost all the backtracking from dead end channels and ledes too close to the Sisters' deadly force had been at the start of their journey. And he'd found Reyna looking at him oddly more than once towards the end. But this unexpected new ability filled him with such joy and pride that he didn't care.

He felt the excitement rise again as he looked back at the Octopus, now almost lost in the darkness, and knew he'd discovered something important on this trip. Something that meant his life would never again be the same.

By the time he stopped gazing at the sunset and followed Reyna into the smoky, savoury-smelling warmth, she'd sold the otter and seal hides they'd collected on their journey – for a good price, judging by her expression, and was part way through a plate of fish stew and a skin of horribly sour wine.

He fetched himself a plate of stew from the cook, a wiry youngster with teeth as brown as the Spindrift's planking, and sat opposite her. Despite the terrible wine, he could tell she was exhilarated at having finally reached the Inn, her dark eyes sparkling as she shovelled in the food, drinking in their surroundings as fast as she was downing the booze.

She topped up both of their cups, raised hers to him. "To you, Jarn," she said, with a suddenly grave expression. He made no answering sign with his own cup, it being bad luck to drink to yourself. "And to the Spindrift," she continued, and now he could raise his wine, first to touch her goblet and then to his lips. He smiled as he drank despite the sourness of the liquid. The Spindrift had certainly proved her worth on their journey. He was almost looking forward to going back east again. Now he'd done it once, he knew it'd be easier. He might even try diving for oysters, if he could get some warming seal grease here at the Inn. He wouldn't want to swim in the cold waters of the Octopus without a protective covering.

And maybe Reyna would stay with him, after the trip back, and they could go into business together – even become partners in life. It was always better to dive with a trusted companion minding the boat up top. And he did trust her now. She'd worked hard during the outward journey to catch game for the pot, skinning and gutting what she shot with her bow or killed with her knife. He'd done some too, of course, but mostly he'd been concentrating on anchoring the Spindrift in channels that didn't look likely to close up on them overnight. So it had been Reyna who'd taken the Spindrift's tender and rowed ashore to hunt, often coming back wet and tired but never empty-handed.

"What are you thinking of?" Reyna asked, and he realised he'd been staring through her for several minutes.

"Oh," he smiled, suddenly embarrassed. "About how it will be easier going home. Now that we know how to do it. We can stay here a few days, stock up with supplies then go back knowing we can. I think... It felt right, Reyna. It felt like I belong here. In the Octopus."

She looked at him oddly for a moment, her cup halfway to her lips, then flashed him a quick smile, finished the motion and swallowed a big gulp of wine.

"It sounds like a good plan," she said. "But first, let's get drunk. Let's get really drunk and celebrate."

And so they did. Reyna seemed to have an inexhaustible capacity for drink; first the horrible wine, then she got to flirting with the barmaid, a skinny young woman with enormous blue eyes. And somehow that led to their next wineskin being filled with something that even from the smell of it Jarn half expected to eat through his cup. Tasted good, though. Or strong, at least.

Shortly after that the music started up, two fiddles and a drum, and singers taking it in turns as they felt inclined, and people began to clap their hands, stamp their feet and eventually to swing each other around in the open area by the bar. Jarn wasn't much good at dancing, but neither were any of the other patrons, or else they'd all been at the spirits too, judging by their tangled steps and laughter, so he joined in with pleasure.

At one point, he and Reyna both made it back to their table at the same time. She'd been dancing with a group of women – some locals, some from the latest dirigible group – and they'd been more rowdy than the men.

She collapsed into her chair, laughing, and removed one of her boots then peeled back the sock beneath to inspect her toes.

"Not broken," she said, wiggling them. "Just felt like it." She bent to replace her boot, and just then a hand crashed down on his back, and Reyna's too, nearly knocking her head into the table, and a man with a salt and pepper beard leaned in between them. He brought with him a strong smell of the sea, even over the scents of cooking, beer and bodies.

"So this is him, is it?" he asked, peering closely at Jarn, then turning to Reyna for confirmation. "This is Ferrin's grandson?"

Reyna looked annoyed, but answered anyway, though with a tone that clearly implied she wasn't in the mood for conversation.

"Ask him yourself. He's got a tongue in his head."

By this time, Jarn wasn't at all sure he could remember how to speak, but the noises he did succeed in producing seemed to satisfy the other man.

"Garek," said the latter, extending a calloused hand. Jarn took it automatically, but found himself suddenly overwhelmed by the memories awoken by that coarse grasp, in such close conjunction with his grandfather's name. Of the old man showing him how to tie knots, how to feel where the wind was coming from, how to read the flow of the water beneath the keel of the boat. And of his father's own rough-skinned fist, seemingly always raised against Jarn no matter what he did.

"Pleased to meet you," he slurred, then shook his head and wished he hadn't, feeling the bile rise. "I'm sorry. I'd best take myself off to bed before the drink makes a fool of me." And he rose to leave.

"Ah, no problem," said Garek heartily, lifting his hand to give Jarn another jovial but crashing blow to the shoulder that almost had him on his knees. "I just stopped to say yer supplies are stowed aboard like we agreed." He presented a key to Reyna – the key, Jarn couldn't help noticing, to Spindrift's galley storage. "I'm away to bed myself. But we can talk tomorrow. Good to see you here, lad. Good to have the Spindrift back among us again." And with that, he disappeared into the crowd, leaving Jarn unsteadily upright and staring at Reyna.

"Damn him," she said with a small laugh, shrugging her shoulders. "I asked him not to say. It was to be a surprise. I did get a very good price for those pelts, so I had Garek restock the Spindrift for us. You weren't supposed to know until it came time for us to set off."

She got up and came around the table and draped her arms around Jarn's neck, pulling his head close to hers and saying, her lips against his ear, "We'll have to find some other way I can surprise you now, won't we?" And he found that he perhaps wasn't as drunk as he'd thought.

Jarn was jolted awake by shouting and the sound of running feet outside, below the window. He cracked open one eye and groaned. It was daylight, but only just. His head felt surprisingly clear, but he knew from past experience that this was likely only temporary. As soon as he was properly awake, the after-effects of the drink would make themselves known with great emphasis. So he resolved not to wake up until the afternoon at the very least. He turned over, intending to pull Reyna close to him and sleep again, but discovered that the other side of the bed was empty, the sheets cold. He barely had time to wonder at this before there were swift steps in the passage outside and someone threw open the door.

"Wh..." he managed.

It was the barmaid, Tara, closely followed by Garek, the room filling quickly with the smell of tar and fish from his clothes and threatening to upset Jarn's stomach all over the scrubbed floorboards.

"See?" she said. "I told you he'd not gone with her."

Garek briefly considered the wretched figure in the bed before striding over to the window. "Aye, so that leaves just the lass then. And she's into Watersmeet proper now, so there's no getting her back."

"Can't you go after her?" asked Tara. And Jarn, his brain finally leaping into action, suddenly realised what they were talking about. Suppressing the aches and the foul taste in his mouth, he struggled out of the tangled sheets and stumbled across to the window, disregarding his nakedness. He elbowed Tara aside, and peered out through the grimy glass.

Beyond the finger of rock and scrubby grass that protected the moorings, the sea was silver blue and smooth as metal in the early morning light. All save a band of rumpled, swirling, unpredictable texture like the crumpled sheet on the floor behind him; Watersmeet, where the Two Sisters came together at the end of the whole continent. A patch of water so hard to read that even seabirds avoided it for fear of sudden whirlpools, air currents and oversized waves. And there, just entering the first small folds of its fabric, was the Spindrift. His Spindrift. His home, his profession – his life. He groaned aloud, and his knees sagged. Garek's strong arm was suddenly around him, holding him up, but not trying to help him back to the bed. The older man knew that Jarn wouldn't look away; couldn't, not while his boat was out there, facing that. Reyna was nothing to him, just a new love like many he'd had before. The finest looking, perhaps – and now he could see why she'd chosen him despite that – but compared to those few strides of wood and rope and iron that together formed his boat...she was nothing.

So he watched as the Spindrift sailed on through the chaotic waters. He'd expected her to plunge and dance, to struggle against the currents and eddies, but she seemed to simply slip over the surface.

Garek voiced aloud what he was thinking. "Aye, well, she has some sense then. She's chosen the right time for it. Low Meet all this moon quarter." He turned to Jarn then, furrowing his brow and asked, "Who was she, lad? Where did she come from? She told me she was from inland, but no inlander ever managed a boat like that. And she knows Watersmeet, at least as much as anyone can know it."

"I..." Jarn still couldn't tear his eyes from his boat, his beautiful boat, as she slid further and further away from him towards the horizon, towards the Brittle Sea. "I don't know who she was, or where she came from. I don't really know anything about her. We just travelled together. Travelled here."

Tara picked up the sheet and draped it over Jarn's shoulders, helping him to wrap it around his shivering form. Then she bent again to the floor, straightening with a piece of paper in her hand. Jarn's eyes were still fixed on the Spindrift, but Garek noticed her movement.

"What have you there?"

"I... a note, maybe? I think it's his name." She gestured at the letters on the front as Garek took the note from her. It was a thick fold of crisp, heavy, yellowish paper with edges that looked somehow organic. Garek peered at the writing on the outside, pointlessly; he'd never learned to read either and for all he knew he had the thing upside down.

He glanced at Jarn, who was still transfixed by the sight of his boat disappearing into the early morning mist that always formed beyond Watersmeet at this time of day. Garek stood and watched too, until the last glimpse of the mast top faded into the milky whiteness, then briskly handed the note to him.

Jarn's fingers took it without conscious instruction, his eyes remaining on the last place he'd seen the Spindrift, willing her to reappear, as if a woman who'd done all this was suddenly going to change her mind and return his ship to him, make his life whole again.

And as his skin brushed the paper, he felt something; a stirring somewhere in his mind, as if a large sea creature had suddenly twisted far below, a roiling of the water bringing hidden currents to the surface. He looked at the note, then, and saw that it was indeed his name on the front. Stefan had been a harsh father but one who'd appreciated the value of education – though Jarn had more than once wondered if that was only so there were more things to punish him for. He opened the fold of paper, and saw that it contained only a single word. At least he thought it was a word, for it was written in a script he had never seen before.

He looked helplessly at Garek and Tara. "I can't...I don't know what it says." And anyway, how could a single word possibly explain why Reyna had done what she had done? How could it express anything that would help him understand?

"Them from the university," said Tara. "In the annexe. That Megan and her friends. Scholars the lot of them, even though they're all women." She sounded disapproving, but determined. "I'll be bound there's one amongst them that can read it."

Jarn dressed rapidly, and they went downstairs, finding the woman named Megan slumped at one of the bench tables in the main taproom, wearing an oversized woollen sweater with complicated cable patterns and staring dubiously at a steaming mug of something with a bitter scent. As she looked blearily up at them, Jarn recognised her from the group that had been doing the most enthusiastic dancing and shouting the previous night.

She ran one hand through her hair and tried to open her eyes fully. "Morning, Tara," she croaked, in a voice rough with too much singing and not enough sleep. "What was all the shouting about earlier? Woke me up. Woke everyone up." She yawned, voluminously, covering her mouth with one sweater-clad hand.

"Good morning to you, Megan," said Tara, sitting down and gesturing to Jarn to do the same. "We have need of your learning."

"Oh yes?" said Megan incuriously, her eyes brushing over Jarn without catching, then returning to her drink. "You interested in magnetism and saline currents, then?"

"Not that," said Tara. "But...here, you'll be able to read this for us, won't you?" she gestured and Jarn presented the note to Megan. And as he moved his hand across the table, with the note open to display the mysterious word, he felt a kind of vibration inside him, like the tilt and shudder of the deck over a dangerously big wave. And he saw Megan's eyes fix on the paper, and widen, and her hands twitch towards her eyes as though to shield them... And then the moment had passed and Megan was staring straight at him, glaring, furious, her hands flat on the table and her mouth working as if she couldn't be sure what she needed to say.

"What?" he asked. "What ails you?"

"You come to me, unannounced, with such a thing" – she nodded at the fold of paper – "and ask what ails me?" Then she seemed to collect herself, taking a couple of deep breaths. "No, you couldn't know, could you?" She bowed her head and sighed deeply, then looked back at them, all three with their eyes wide and curious. "Is it yours?" She indicated the note.

"Left for me," said Jarn bitterly. And Tara and Garek explained briefly what Reyna had done, while Jarn sat in embarrassment between them on the bench.

"Yes," said Megan when they'd finished speaking. "Left for you. Well. You'll remember now."

"Remember? I...what?"

"Not yet." She took a deep breath. "Now." And then she spoke a word. The word, Jarn wondered, on the paper?

And at the sound of her voice, he did indeed remember. He remembered how the trip had really gone. He remembered who Reyna had really been. He knew why she had left the note. And what it was.

All had been as he thought until some way into the archipelago. At the start of the journey he'd taken little notice of what she'd brought for the pot, simply being grateful for food after a day of effort and concentration, seeking the way through the Octopus. But as he began to feel the way and navigation became easier, he offered to go with her on her hunting trips. She always refused. "I'm better on my own," she said. But there was a something in her manner of saying it that made him wonder. He found himself watching her even more closely after that. Her, her weapons, her preparations. And finally, her kills.

And he saw, as she brought the game into the camp for butchering and to remove the skin for drying, that none of her prey had wounds. At least, none visible – no cuts, no areas of discoloured fur or feather where she could feasibly have brought them down with a stone.

So one day he waited until Reyna had disappeared out of sight in the tender, behind a large island some distance away, and he quickly brought out the folding coracle he'd bought on an impulse in Lulworth the previous winter, and paddled after her.

As he'd discovered when he first used the coracle, it was a rather damp and strenuous means of transport. But eventually he spotted the tender, pulled up onto the root tangles and low dark berry plants fringing another islet. There was no sign of Reyna, and he was beginning to think he'd have to turn around and go back none the wiser when he noticed a faint but fresh trail through the vegetation.

After a few minutes, as he skirted a clump of stunted trees, he caught sight of her through the sparse leaves, stock still like a hunting dog. And beyond her, also still but clearly just about to flee, was a teyjak – the small, almost wine-coloured deer native to the Octopus.

For a moment all three of them were motionless and silent, heavy with potential, like the limpid sea before a storm. And then, suddenly, shockingly, Reyna spoke – shouted. He didn't catch the words themselves, but even with her back to him he felt the impact of their force like a heavy blow to the chest, knocking him to the ground. No, not his chest – his very heart. He could feel it thumping, flopping about like a gaffed fish unable to set itself to rights. He resisted the strong urge to cough his guts up onto the cool green leaves beneath his hands and knees, and as soon as he could move again he did so, half-stumbling back towards the coracle.

He didn't bother to look back to see if she'd spotted him. He was pretty sure that even if she hadn't, he wouldn't be able to keep the knowledge of what she was off his face.

Wordwitch.

The title kept running through his head, emerging from his deepest childhood memories like a treacherous rock for an unwary keel. He recalled his grandmother telling him a story of a boy who'd met a Wordwitch and insulted her somehow, and so she'd spelled him into thinking he could fly. He'd plummeted from a cliff and dashed himself into pieces on the rocks below. And the Wordwitch had laughed and walked away, changing her appearance with a word as she went. Jarn's grandmother had warned him that a Wordwitch could put a spell on you without you even knowing it, just by giving you a piece of paper or writing something on a wall with a piece of charcoal. But his father had laughed and accused her of being superstitious and just trying to excuse the fact that she'd never gone to school and was distrustful of writing.

And as he'd grown up, Jarn had assumed that his grandmother's stories of Wordwitches had been just that. But now he knew the truth.

He remembered, now, Reyna getting back to the Spindrift, pulling the tender alongside and calling to him just like normal to help her bring her catch up on deck. He remembered her face. Not angry, not even the cool amusement he'd grown used to from her; unexpectedly, she looked embarrassed. Ashamed, even.

And when she climbed back aboard, she softly said his name and hesitantly took him by the arm.

"I'm sorry, Jarn. But you should not have followed me."

Jarn snorted and pulled his arm away. "Aye, well I see that now. Could you not have put a word on me to stop me doing so?"

"Don't be angry with me," she said. "It was best you didn't know. My kind have suffered enough that we don't announce our presence without good reason."

And later that night, as they ate the venison, she told him of the Wordwitches. Stories to match those of his grandmother. Stories from the other side of the fence, of persecution and cruelty and hatred aimed at women who just happened to have a knack with words.

"But women can be scholars now," he protested. "Women are accepted by the universities. There's no need to hide yourselves now."

"*Rich* women can be scholars," she corrected him. "It's just like your Skyborn and Waterborn. Some are allowed anything, no matter their gender. Money smoothes the way for them. But a learned woman who is not of wealthy family? No. We'd still be outcasts wherever people knew us."

"You could do good," he insisted stubbornly. "You could help people. You could make a difference. Then you'd be accepted."

She became angry then, eyes flashing. "You think we don't do that already? You think we don't already help our communities, unseen, unknown? Do you think we don't talk of a time when we can carry out our profession openly?"

He opened his mouth to say something else, but she cut him off with a gesture. "I had a friend who thought like you. She'd lived in her village all her life. Her mother had been a Wordwitch before her, and her mother before that... Her family had always lived there, for hundreds of years. And so Allryn decided she'd be safe. Because she was one who said, like you, that if we were useful to people they'd accept us. That it was time." Reyna shook her head. "Do you know what they did? The day, the same day, that she told the head man? He came to her house with his daughter, who she'd saved from the fever by driving out the badness with a Word. And he slit his own daughter's throat in front of her, out on the road. And the child's blood ran into the dust and pooled at Allryn's feet. And after that, she just let them take her. They did the same to her, then burned her house and left the blackened ruins as a reminder, with her head on a stake outside."

Jarn wanted to say she was lying, but he knew she wasn't. He knew he was naive in many ways, despite his years at sea, but he'd encountered enough cruelty and spite to understand that people really did act so inhumanely to each other.

"I'm sorry," he said, and he put one hand over hers where it rested on the galley table. "It must be hard to be so disliked just for being able to do something other people can't."

She looked at him then, steadily, for a few moments, then stared down at the Spindrift's table as if she was calculating something. And then she looked back up at him and spoke another Word that made him forget.

When he came back to himself, he was in one of the Inn's side rooms, lying on a padded bench.

"...be leaving later today, and he's welcome to take passage with us," a woman's voice was saying nearby. A man replied, but the conversation seemed to be moving away from him, or perhaps he was slipping back into unconsciousness again.

Footsteps approached, and he smelled something warm and savoury. And he opened his eyes to Tara, holding a bowl of stew and smiling to see him awake again. Then the memories broke over him again, leaving him gasping for air. He lurched upright, and Tara stepped back rapidly, nearly spilling the food.

"Sorry," he said. "I'm sorry, I'm just...I thought..." He rubbed the back of his neck. "I don't even know what I thought. How am I going to get home? What will I even do when I get there, without a boat? Trading's all I know."

"I'm thinking you have no need to fret about that," said Tara, proffering the bowl. "Eat this first. It'll do you good."

He took it from her and found that it did indeed help him feel a little more human at least, a little less disconnected from his surroundings. By the time he'd scooped up the last mouthful, he felt once more like he belonged in his body, that his clothes and skin were the right size, rather than foreign things threatening to overturn his composure with every minor chafing movement.

He stood up slowly, and when that seemed to be working too, he went slowly out into the passage outside, and then into the taproom, taking the empty bowl with him. He placed it down on the counter in front and waited for Tara, who was serving ale to another customer. When she came over, he gestured to the bowl and said, "You were right, it did help. What do I owe you? I do have a few coins left." He went to open the pouch at his belt, but Tara waved it away.

"Don't be foolish. You were robbed under our roof; we're not the type to kick you when you're down. You can pay me back by bringing some sisak root next time you're here. No matter how many times I ask the dirigible crews for it, they always forget. Or bring me sassirak instead, and that makes the stew too bitter."

"I'd willingly bring you any amount of sisak root, but I'll never be back here again," he gestured to the room, then pointed out of the window. "In fact, I'll probably never be able to *leave* here again. Not without a boat."

"Typical man," said a voice beside him, and Megan smiled at his confusion as she continued. "Always exaggerating the tiniest setback into a disaster." Behind her, Garek snorted in amusement, but she held up one hand as Jarn began to protest. "No, you won't be stuck here; you can come back on our dirigible when we leave tomorrow. In the meantime you can help me take measurements of the magnetic flow. It's boring work and it'll be much quicker with someone to help."

"I...thank you," Jarn said, not having the faintest idea what that would involve but grateful all the same. That was indeed a weight from his shoulders. Something to occupy him now and a way back home. Once back in Capstone he'd be able to find some way of rebuilding his life. There were people who owed him, small favours that had mounted up over the years since he'd been in business for himself.

"And I can sort you out with a boat, lad," said Garek. "No need to make me that face, I mean what I say! I know someone in Capstone, old Liam Farilly, he's looking to retire but he has no kin and he'd be happy for his boat to go to someone who'll care for it. I dare say he'll expect a cut of your cargoes for a while, but you won't be the loser by it. The Water Sprite's a fine vessel, and she's used to the waters of the Octopus too. Because you're one of us, lad. Ferrin's grandson belongs here at the Inn."

Jarn opened his mouth to speak, then he looked around at their expectant, grinning faces, and then down at the bar, where a tankard of ale seemed to have magically appeared before each of them, and he shook his head. He'd gone to bed last night with a woman in his life, and a boat and a new trading route and now...he'd lost his boat, never had the woman as it turned out, but he still had the trade and maybe something more...? A place in the world that was really his, not just a set of temporary halts?

"That sounds...very good of you, all of you," he said. "Thank you. I'm very grateful."

"I'll drink to that," said Megan, raising her tankard. Garek and Tara did the same.

"The only thing is..." said Jarn, and the others replaced their drinks on the bar, looking expectantly at him.

"I just feel stupid. I feel like I don't deserve your help. Renya, she just used me, and I should have seen that. She just wanted the Spindrift, that's all. Not me. She must have despised me," he concluded miserably.

"Ha!" barked Megan.

Jarn looked at her stonily. "What?"

"She didn't despise you at all. She must have thought quite a lot of you, actually. She certainly listened to your tales of your father and grandfather. Because she left you this." She drew Reyna's note out from her pocket.

"So? A piece of paper? A magic spell to make me remember now that she's gone and taken everything of mine with her?"

Megan gave a bark of laughter. "Of course, you don't know what the word means, do you?"

He carried on glaring at her.

"The word," Megan went on patiently. "The word she left you, the word that's already started working in your life..." She gestured to Garek and Tara, to herself, indicating somehow in that small flick of her fingers all they'd done for him, everything they had promised to do, and happily so.

"Yes?"

"The word. The word she left for you. It's..." She paused, took another deep breath, then smiled, shaking her head.

"The word is...Family."

The Extra Bit

Thank you so much for reading my stories!

If you enjoyed this book, please give it a review on Goodreads, Amazon or wherever you like to help other people find great books. I know writing a review can be difficult, but if you could take the time to write even a few words I'd be so grateful. Reviews really help self-published authors.

Writing Challenge

If you've always wanted to write but never quite managed to start – or finish – anything, why not try the same challenge that helped me create this book?

Pick a book off your shelf. Any book, although novels are probably easiest.

Randomly choose a set of page numbers and write them down (do this before you open the book, so you don't cheat and pick interesting looking ones!) Then turn to those pages and take a photo of each page with your phone. If it turns out there are no words on a particular page, turn to the next page, or the one before.

Set yourself a target – this can be "I'm going to write for 15 minutes a day when I get up in the morning" or "I'm going to write on the bus to work, however long that takes" or "I'm going to write for 5 minutes in the car waiting to pick the kids up from school." Doesn't matter, as long as it's a duration you can manage. It can be three days a week, all seven or the first Tuesday of the month. You can plan to write by hand, on your phone, on a computer. All three. Any way you want.

Then, at the appointed time, bring up the photo with today's page on it, and pick a word. Don't think too hard about your choice. Just let your eyes drift over the image.

When you've picked your word, take a couple of deep breaths while you let it percolate into your brain, and...start writing.

Don't worry too much about spelling or the exact word if you can't quite remember it. You can leave blanks and look things up later.

You can write for *longer* than you planned, but you can't stop before the end of the time.

You may find a whole story just pops into your head. You may just have a sentence or a character or an event. Doesn't matter what it is, just write it down and let it flow from there.

If you really can't think of anything, write down the letters of the word and rearrange them until something comes into your head. Or just write that word, over and over, until you're so annoyed with it that you start picturing a character doing the same thing and you wonder how they got to that point and...

Happy writing!

The Daisy Chain prompts

And if you're really nosy, and you want to know which words I used to produce the stories – or you want to see where your imagination takes you from the same words – here they are*.

Angel
Baked
Bread
Butter
Calming
Candles
Cheery
Fortune
Ginger
Honey

Little
Market
Musical
Nettle
Potted
Sparkle
Tree
Weather
Yourself

*The observant reader will notice there are only 19, even though I started with 24 prompts, and that's because I'm saving some for the next book! The *incredibly* observant reader will notice that the result of one of the above prompts is in the "And Other Stories" section, because it came out in a different style to the Manx pieces.

Made in the USA
Monee, IL
20 December 2023

50284186R00105